MOVING KINGS

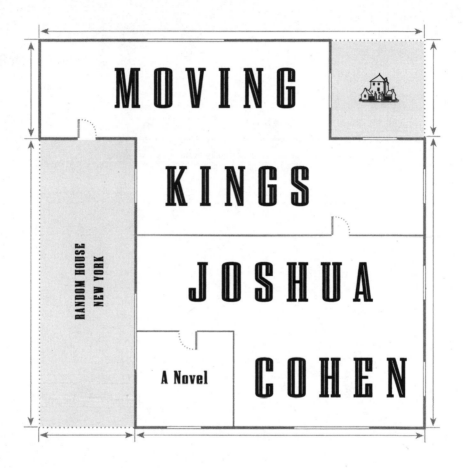

MOVING

KINGS

JOSHUA

COHEN

A Novel

RANDOM HOUSE
NEW YORK

Moving Kings is a work of fiction. Names, characters, places, and incidents either are the product of the author's imagination or are used fictitiously. Any resemblance to actual persons, living or dead, events, or locales is entirely coincidental.

Copyright © 2017 by Joshua Cohen

All rights reserved.

Published in the United States by Random House, an imprint and division of Penguin Random House LLC, New York.

RANDOM HOUSE and the HOUSE colophon are registered trademarks of Penguin Random House LLC.

LIBRARY OF CONGRESS CATALOGING-IN-PUBLICATION DATA

Names: Cohen, Joshua.
Title: Moving kings : a novel / Joshua Cohen.
Description: First Edition. | New York : Random House, [2017]
Identifiers: LCCN 2016052928 | ISBN 9780399590184 (hardback) |
ISBN 9780399590191 (ebook)
Subjects: | BISAC: FICTION / Literary. | FICTION / Jewish. |
FICTION / Political.
Classification: LCC PS3553.O42434 M68 2017 |
DDC 813/.54—dc23
LC record available at lccn.loc.gov/2016052928

Printed in the United States of America on acid-free paper

randomhousebooks.com

987654321

FIRST EDITION

Book design by Simon M. Sullivan

To BC, DC, *and* MC

MOVING KINGS

כִּי הֶחֱרַשְׁתִּי בָּלוּ עֲצָמָי בְּשַׁאֲגָתִי כָּל הַיּוֹם:

[Because I didn't speak up my bones wore old
through roaring all the day.]
—PSALM 32

DAVID
(In Distraint)

YE shall know them by their vehicles: those blue trucks that're always cutting you off on your way to the airport, sides emblazoned with grimy white crowns, dinged bumpers stickered GOT A PROBLEM WITH MY DRIVING? CALL 1-800-212-KING!

Ye shall know them by their ads: on basic cable and drive-time radio, those billboards that're always blocking the signs and making you miss the airport turn, with their offers of free estimates over the phone and 100% money back guarantees.

Or maybe, like more than 180,000 other satisfied customers served in all five of the boroughs and three neighboring states since 1948, you know them as the Courtly Couriers®, or the Royal Treatment Pros®, or the Removalists with the Regal Touch™—whom you've let into your home, to move your most precious possessions to your new home, or else to one of their six 24-hour, security-monitored, climate-controlled storage facilities conveniently located throughout the New York Metropolitan Area.

Or maybe, whatever you know is wrong, because you've just been reading their online reviews.

King's Moving (David King, President, Spokesman, Container of Crises, Stresses, & the Distrained) was a licensed, bonded, limited-liability insured large small business that specialized in—one guess—moving . . . 'n' storage . . . 'n' parking . . . 'n' towing . . . 'n' salvage . . . 'n' scrap, activities that demanded the bloodsweat of plus/minus 40 fulltime and 60 parttime employees, 50 vehicles, three lots, five garages, six 24-hour, security-monitored, climate-controlled storage facilities conveniently located throughout the New York Metropolitan Area—not to mention a headquarters in Jersey City, hard by the piers.

Above all, King's Moving was a family business. Family owned, family operated. Family, family, family . . . Take that into account, Your Honor . . .

It was summer, toward the weekend of a holiday week—Moving Day (last day of the month, first day of the month), followed by Independence Day—and David King was out in the Hamptons at a birthday party for America, to which he'd been invited as a member of the Empire Club, which had required attendees to donate upwards of $4K for the privilege of drinking diluted booze and eating oversauced BBQ under the auspices of the New York State Republican Committee.

Inviting him to a party and then making him pay: that was class. That was how billionaires stayed billionaires.

And David, who'd resented even the toll to the Long Island Expressway, couldn't help but wonder whether he'd met $4K worth of people yet—he couldn't help valuating everything: the people, the property, the Victorianized manse shadowing the pool. His phone was vibrating again in his pocket.

He canceled the call—he was working.

He was working by attending a party at which he didn't know anyone, or knew only that he recognized: names, faces, profiles.

It was work having to restrain himself from mentioning mergers he'd only read about, acquisitions that weren't his, a celebrity stranger's divorce/custody negotiations still ongoing— having to endure discussions of clean ocean and beach replenishment initiatives, when all he wanted to know was: daughter or wife? when all he wanted to know was: does anyone know where our host is? It was work pretending he blended, he mixed, pretending he wasn't sweating and had a second residence of his own and was a Hamptons vet and agreeing yes hasn't the Meadow Lane heliport gotten so crowded lately? and yes isn't Ray from Elite Landscapers just the best?

Because the fact remained that David had never been this far out on the Island before and not only couldn't he tell you which of the Hamptons he was in, he couldn't even tell you the number of Hamptons, or the differences between the Hamptons, or what made a Hampton a Hampton, singular, to begin with.

"Hope we're not keeping you?" a lady said.

David said, "Come again?"

"You keep checking your phone."

"I've got foreign business, never stops. It's already July 5th somewhere."

And he excused himself from that bezant of lawn and its assembly of skinny flagpole women flying dresses in red, white, and blue.

Ruth, his office manager, had been calling without leaving messages. Now she was gibberish txting: *sorry sorry bill sick have take bill jr bball practice.*

And then: *anyway not finding passcard.*

David made his way among tents, buffet tables of chafing and carving and bars—the trick was to keep on the move.

Kids—put David around kids and he'd fantasize about having them and only then would he recall that he had a daughter, who was an adult now—the kids were having their faces smeared native with warpaint. They bounced around on a giant inflatable galleon, parried and thrust with balloon swords.

A breeze blew in with the dung of elephant rides.

He moved among servers who made $8.75 an hour and so who made about 14 cents, 14.5833 cents, he did the figures in his head, for each minute it took them to carve him primerib or fix him a scotch or direct him and his menthols to a smoking area.

Conversations collected, as they were conducted, in circles. About stocks, about realestate, stocks. About renovations and how draining it was to open a house for the season. Apparently, to have two houses meant always neglecting one of them, at least. About alarm systems, sprinkler systems, sump pumps, white vs. black mold. About politics.

David's politics were aspirational, inferior: he was in favor of contacts, contracts, the right to not diet, and the right to jump lines at dessert stations.

David King was a man who if a longtime employee flaked on a commitment on short notice because her exhusband was too

ill to take their son to a baseball practice that wasn't even hard-
ball but actually softball, or if his primerib came closer to medium than to the already spineless concession that was medium
rare, or if his Dewar's 18 turned out to be Dewar's 15 or 12 or
God forbid came with an icecube or even just an extra splash of
water, or if the line for the dessert station was moving so inde-
cisively slowly that his icecream would melt before he got to
the toppings he liked—it wasn't his fault that he was so decisive
about his toppings—he'd scream, he'd have a conniption, and
yet once he'd fudged his sundae with a cherry atop he had all
the attention, all the guilty sated childlike attention, for being
lectured by an Ivy League B student on the new model Gulf-
streams (though David didn't have his own plane), the best sail-
ing routes (though David didn't have his own boat), the best
steeplechase courses (David didn't even have a pony), how
New York State was the most regulated state in the union, the
state with the highest taxes, the state with the highest energy
costs, the highest fuel costs, the highest insurance premiums,
and a convoluted body of tort law that made even the Nazi jus-
tice system seem unbiased and lenient, and how so and so was
really the only candidate to bet on, so and so the only candidate
who had real plans both for the Middle East and for midsized
American businesses (our composited Ivy League B student
apparently knew his audience)—the only candidate who was
legitimately "Pro-Growth," and that was the line, or the jargon,
that struck him, and brought to mind the image of a small mod-
est neat building, like some fourfloor prewar walkup in the Village, which with every vote for a Republican grew taller by the
floor, until it became this big shiny tower that clockhanded all
of Manhattan, and then, by association, his mind flashed below

his belt, which was on its last notch, and below his gut, which hung like a panting tongue over it, to his bloodless dick, which—as if his heart had betrayed the party platform, "Pro-Growth"—dangled limp and useless.

It was distressing—to others, but not to himself, who didn't notice—how he'd change. How he'd let himself be lectured, talked down to. How he'd become, in certain situations, not servile exactly, but docile, tamed. A Jew. And so he'd always wind up thanking his interlocutor for the condescension, for the aeronautical, nautical, equestrian, or civic education. Just like after he'd shout at Ruth, he'd apologize and give her a raise, just like he'd always overtip his servers—even tipping them at an event like this, where accepting gratuities would get them in trouble.

David's normal social calendar had him visiting precincts, firehouses, and school auditoria, cultivating such notable personalities as: Port Authority commissioner, State Assembly member, City Council member, Borough president, Borough Board member, Community Board member, the executive of the Teamsters Locals 560 and 831, and of the DOB, DCP, DOT, and DSNY. This occasion, however, was mayoral and beyond—it was congressional and beyond—the developers, the financiers, the waspiest machers, robust with exemptions, strong in abatements. The people who ran the energy companies, not the people who ran the fuel distribution depots and waste disposal services. The bankers who drove the interest rates and generals who earned medals, not the retired cops who drove the armored cars and former hacks who owned medallions. Mingling with this class had gotten him awkward, apprehensive. With his side of the mouth talking, his talking hands, checking his fly with sticky fingers.

All his struggles were in his face. All his personas in combat: king, commoner, selfmade, incomplete. The booze and red meat and dairy. The pills ostensibly for bloodpressure and the pills ostensibly for cholesterol and the pills he wasn't sure what they did: for anxiety. He didn't swear by anything, just swallowed it. He never knew what to say, or knew but got his audiences crossed, got lost in the game, playing against type when he should've been playing to type, playing to when he should've been playing against. Golf with racquet sports enthusiasts and racquet sports with golfers. With a Belgian diplomat he'd discussed the chance of rain. With the CEO of a cosmetics firm he'd discussed how most people think the Iranians are Arabs. It didn't help that most people here considered it obnoxious to mention, or to be pressured into mentioning, what they did for a living, which was who they were for a living, so that actors and actresses and uniformed military personnel aside, the only presences here whose identities were in any way legible to him were the servers, so he bantered with them, about why he was refusing to support an increase in the minimum wage, and whether or not they'd seen the host of the party, and then he'd tuck singles into their pockets and tell them to tell him if they heard anything. What he was, then, was local color, just out of his locale. They probably thought he was physically tough. They probably thought he was in with the mob.

David edged his way around the crowd, which pressed in around the dancefloor, at the center of which a professional couple of professional dancers swung and hopped and twirled.

Keys, guitar, bass, and drums were locked into a jazz that turned the whole world into an elevator, the horn section rose and riffed. Makeshift baffles to either side of the bandstand held massive eagle art for raffle. The band became a drumroll, which became clapping, as the emcee made a quip about being black and then introduced the candidate.

David was already out—by the beach, an open balmy vista. Bright water, bright sand. Given the winds, it took many changes of stance, many deli matches, to light his kingsized Newport. Then he hefted his phone and dialed Ruth.

"Hello?"

"Ruthie."

"David—hello? Are you driving?"

"Just talk. What's the issue?"

"I can barely—if you're driving, put up the window."

"I'm outside—there's no window outside." He cupped the phone, "What's up?"

"I told you. I can't go."

"Can't or won't?"

"I'm not feeling so hot."

"I thought it was Bill, I thought Bill Jr. Now you're ditzing up your excuses."

"No excuses."

"You seriously don't have it in you to just stock a fridge, bring over the kitchenware and like a blanket or whatever?"

"I've got a son with a playoff game and an exhusband stubborn and vomiting."

"It's just the basics, Ruthie."

"Better you let Paul take care of it."

"Paul's not domestic, he's not even housebroken. And anyway he already did me enough of a favor with the furniture, when he moved out the Bengalis."

"Bangladeshis."

"They leave it decent? You were supposed to clean."

"I'm standing in my exhusband's house, standing in my exhusband's vomit, and feeling woozy myself."

"This is a you and your Bills' problem, but you've made it a you and me problem. And you're fucking over my cousin."

"Fuck you, David. I'm going."

"You mean you're going out there now?"

"I mean I'm pressing the red and hanging up on you."

This was what happened when you relied on an office manager still entangled with her ex, or when you used to screw your office manager still entangled with her ex—the sands kept shifting, the loyalties got kinked like kelp and baited tackle. A barge floated by, laden with fireworks, and David flicked his cig in its direction as if hoping for a gust that would carry the butt ass over ember out over the water and ignite a fuse.

He stomped back through the party (grabbing a bourboned punch), crunched the clamshell drive to the front of the property (leaving his glass in the grass). A valet took his ticket and smirked, "What kind car? Bentley or Rolls?"

David said, "You know what kind. A van, cabron. A Plymouth Estupido."

Two men were approaching, but just as they were about to take the slate steps for the manse, one paused: "Holy shit— holy shit—David King, is that you? David King The Moving King Will Move Your Mothertrucking Everything?"

The man, swimfit in a slimcut suit, loosened necktie toweled around his neck, pumped David's hand: "That was classic. Just a total classic."

He said to his companion, "I was clerking down in DC, but I was always coming back to New York to visit Peg," and then he said to David, "My wife."

The man broke the shake to rub his forehead, go wistful: "Anyway, she'd be going to sleep early, Peg would, she was still doing the morning show then, WFAN, so I'd be up late at night alone, just me and my briefs and Channel J—you know Channel J? Was it only in the city? Public access. Madness. 1-900 partylines, psychic chatshows, neighborhood forums you called into with bulletins that advised about blizzards or where your polls were. None of it exists anymore. You had this one commercial where a family's sitting around a table, mother and daughter talking about their day with the father sitting up at the head on a throne, and the movers come in and just pick him up and take him away and they do it so slick, nobody notices— that was great. That was your own family, David? I always had the feeling. How are they?"

David smiled tight—he was vain. Since that commercial, since he'd dumped that wife, he'd gotten hair implants and replaced his teeth.

He said, "Family's fine, thanks. But I've done a lot since. What about you? Staying awake with any of my new spots?"

The man laughed and his companion said, "So you enjoyed the speech, I gather? The Senator can count on your vote?"

David tried to feign that he'd been joking, telling the Senator, "Sorry, Senator, I was joking."

The Senator said, "Of course," and nodded to his companion, who hadn't laughed. "Let me introduce you to our host."

The hand that now shook David's belonged, like so much else in New York, to Fraunces Bower—of the Corn Exchange, Dodgemoor Estates, 1 Bryant, and 388 Greenwich Bowers, the redeveloper of Roosevelt and Governors Islands and the coowner of Rockefeller Center Bowers—the same Bowers who'd strewn shoppingcenters and subsidized housingprojects across every borough of the city and held all that paper on so many acres of distressed property out in the bleak reaches that if that superfluity of land were ever strung together, contiguous, and dropped on Manhattan, it'd cover Central Park.

Fraunces Bower, who was properly Fraunces Bower III—now installed as principal of Bower Asset Management—was tall and thinlimbed, thinframed, in seersucker. A ray of sun put a shine on his head that prevented David from gauging the degree of his baldness.

"Pleased to meet you, Mr. Bower."

"Fraunces, please," he said and kept wringing David's hand like he was going to make a glove out of it.

The Senator said, "Your chariot awaits."

And so it did, there was no denying: that bruised blue van, its white letters molting, KIN OVING.

The valet jingled the keys, as David took out his wallet and chose among bills: a single or hundreds. He chose $100.

There wasn't any traffic—no one was heading his direction, no one would ever. Because his direction was a circle, or would be, counterclockwise, looping him cross-Island, Queens to

Brooklyn, Manhattan then Jersey, only to turn back around again, Brooklyn to Queens.

Or else he'd drive up from Jersey and hazard Staten Island.

A punitive, regurgitative route. Thanks Ruthie. He was still slightly drunk and it felt like rain. He put a cig in his mouth just to suck.

Waiting at a light, before the bridge into Manhattan, he checked his phone: his cousin's flight had just departed, on time.

A guy stood out by the turn to Canal Street—neither a vendor nor a squeegeeist, and if he seemed not just jobless but also homeless in abscess and rags he didn't seem to be panhandling, though he held a cardboard boxflap sign, SAVE THE HUDSON, and then flipped it around, PAVE THE HUDSON, and then flipped it again—and David wondered whether this wasn't just another candidate campaigning, and whether the opposing sides of the sign weren't the same: you saved a river by paving it over, letting the water flow beneath untouched.

He raised his window.

To emerge from the tunnel was to be born again, soaked in the sullage of the marshes—coming out headfirst past Liberty and Ellis Islands, *Where it all began*, as David liked to remark to himself, as if that were the wetlands' brand, even though that's not *Where it all began*, because David's father had arrived in the States only after the war, and while Liberty had loitered on her soggy corner immortally, Ellis had already been mothballed and the boat that'd brought his father had docked in Jersey. Exit 14A, David was always accelerating into turns. He lowered his window again, lowered all the windows, to get the stench, the way the methane rushed in like a fart. Port Jersey to

Colony Road: a sparsely lit and sodden strip joining reedy islets, which you'd only drive if you owned or worked for a business located on it or were lost, slowly sinking into the darkness. The desolation stifled, especially in heat. To the right were the yards, their shippingcontainers like bulky ridged cinderblocks stacked into barracks, so many of the blues from Korea, but lately more of the German greens, the Chinese reds and yellows. To the left were the piers, their solemn cranes saluting the tankers slipping by. Below, down in the murk, that's where you got rid of the murders and of the guns that turned people into murders. That's where your hotwired Buick was ditched, in an underwater parkinglot of broken boilers, leaky microwaves, and all the AA batteries.

Toward the end of the strip was King's HQ, girded by barbedwire.

David dug out his asswarmed wallet, for his passcard. He should never have given one to Ruth. But if not Ruth, who else should have one? Because who else, if the worst happened, would make sure his daughter was taken care of?

His daughter. Not Ruth's.

He hung himself out the window, swiped the slab across the sensor, the gate slid along its track.

Harsh bugswarmed LED luminaires, grate stairs to an office of pitted brick, from which the warehouses extended like trust into the dimming.

Tim Brynks, AKA Tinks, was behind the desk, fixed in the chair, fixated on screens: one was showing porn, the other five the feeds from the CCTV.

David said, "Sorry to interrupt your jerkoff session."

Tinks didn't break from his screen: "I don't jerkoff."

"Here you don't?"

"Ever I don't."

"Bullshit."

"No bullshit," and Tinks twitched, swiveled. "I like the tension of not, it keeps me awake—I like how they don't talk."

David went to the minifridge, got them both Tecates.

"You're in the office why? Your computer down at home?"

David chugged and grimaced. "To be honest," he said, "I never understood anything with a dick in it."

How it worked was that you signed a contract—a bill of lading. Which asserted that you assumed sole risk, and that you and your heirs, successors, executors, and subrogates did hereby agree to waive and release, indemnify and hold harmless, King's Moving, Inc., its directors, officers, employees, and agents, from and against any and all claims, actions, causes of actions, and suits for accidental and/or negligent damage and/or loss.

Then, you packed up your belongings and moved, or had your belongings packed up and moved for you, to the nearest King's Moving facility, to one of the blue and white precast blights in Manhattan (Downtown), Manhattan (Uptown), Brooklyn, Queens, Staten Island, the Bronx, and there they remained, there they reposed: all your outgrown babyclothes, strollers, and cribs, all your iceskates, woks, and blenders. But then say you changed your address and forgot to give notice and so fell behind on payments. Because of alimony expenses. Because of health expenses. Say you went bankrupt or to prison or just died. After six months of notifications of delinquency with interest calculated, followed by a two month grace period during which the accounting department, Ruth, would attempt to trace and bill your next of kin—who'd never be found, or if found would typically refuse or be unable to pay arrears—all your junk would be transferred here, and ownership reverted, as King's Moving moved to recoup its losses.

This facility, Jersey City, kept the spoils: your possessions re-possessed, stored inside concrete pillboxes wallowing in septic and brine.

The first warehouse's units still hadn't been processed and so were tagged to lot, which was freaky: they were like miniature theaters, shrinkydink stage sets. Behind their metal curtains were rooms, which were filled with other rooms: there was a 1950s livingroom (eggchair, boomerang table), neighboring a 1970s den (heavy on the teak), across the hall from a summer 1984 recroom in mintcondition replete with astroturf, a nauga-hyde La-Z-Boy, and a pennant from the LA Olympics—all of them containing all of the furnishings and effects of their origi-nating locations, but just crowded now, cluttered up, because the units were small: 20' × 20', 15' × 15', 10' × 10'. You almost expected to find the people inside. Instead you just found hints, intimations, material vestiges of mind: hubcaps, a welding rig, a treadmill, a sybian saddle. Each unit had its drama. Each was an inventory of an absent person's life, all the stuff they hadn't been able to live with, but weren't prepared to lose: a unit of eviscerated photoalbums with snapshots skittering the floor, another totally vacant except for a roofless dollhouse.

The second warehouse's units had already been processed and so were tagged to item, which was easier to deal with: they weren't as human. The units just of shelving arranged haphaz-ardly wall to wall, the units packed to the ceiling's sprinklers with chests, the unit of stray drawers. Things, deprived of their relationships with their owners, and even of their relationships with their owners' other things, were now just related to one another. To others of their kind. They'd been restored to their kind, and so sterilized, laundered, mended. Lamps among lamps. Stereo components among stereo components. This made them simpler to price and post online, in the hopes of bypassing the resalers and selling the hutchdesks and loveseats and teddybears direct to the hutchdesk and loveseat and teddybear collectors.

Down the way was the unit of clocks, from whose shutter came a raspy crippled ticking.

David swiped through to the third warehouse—letting the fluorescents sense his motion and flick on, letting them flicker and thrum along with the echoes of his pacing. Towels, linens. Bowls and plates. That's what the house still lacked: the little domiciliary niceties.

He was trying to think what they were—what his parents'd had. What he'd had. The appliances of childhood. If he found even half that stuff, that would be enough for his cousin.

He found a wheeled pallet, piled it with flatware and stemware. He had no qualms about breaking up the sets. The sets were incomplete already. Anyway, how many knives did one guy need? How many pots and pans? He took six placesettings, figuring his cousin wouldn't be too keen on doing dishes. He took three waterglasses, three wineglasses, and then this gleaming soup tureen whorled like a shell and capacious enough to bathe a baby in. He swaddled it in tablecloth, settled it on the pallet. It was stupid to have asked Ruth to do this. Ruth who'd been trying to get him to commit to her forever. Ruth who'd been trying to get him to settle. To have asked her to pick out everything, but the correct everything, to basically shop for a home, which would never be their home, was cruel. Still, she would've known what to get, she would've known what was appropriate. Like, what to do if his cousin kept kosher? Wouldn't he need all this same stuff again, but separate? David backtracked, out of prudence and—automatically considering the plain porcelain and aluminum utensils more appropriate for dairy—took more lidded pots and a fryingpan for meat, meat knives with faux wood handles, and meat bowls and plates wreathed in ivy.

All that stooping to lift the shutters, to lift the loads, he ached. His goddamned lumbars.

He chocked the heaped pallet against an interior door, tapped dates into the keypad: the year his Tammy was born, followed by the year he left, or was left by, his wife. The lights here he had to toggle himself, without tripping. Black boxes hindered the way, black safes hoarded into corners. Racks of purses and leather jackets, cold storage lockers roaring with furs, the skins he'd claimed shivering on hangers. He'd gather here, annually or so, with his experts from the city. Deviants into coins and stamps and sports memorabilia, who'd pick through the bins of autographed jerseys, bats, and balls. Also, this cranky provenancer from Amish country Pennsylvania who was the leading authority on Civil War tchotchkes.

Once there'd been an urn that wound up being Egypt, New Kingdom, ca. 14th–13th century BCE, appraised at $400K, and it went for $620K, at auction.

The jewelry was in the wall.

He turned to the camera bracketed midwall and considered draping a sheet, but why should he be embarrassed? Why shouldn't Tinks be?

He waved at Tinks. Give my regards to the lesbians.

He swiped at the vault and then keyed in the same years but reversed: his splitdate and then the birthdate, Tammy's. Inside were trays, dark and softly cushioned.

He took a pendant necklace, let it unspool loose in his pocket.

From there, it was a hustle down the ramp to the yard, to the maintenance shed to snag a bucket and mop, then it was pushing the pallet, kicking its casters realigned and through the mire—he realized only halfway there it would've been better to've left the pallet at the top of the ramp and just backed the van on up to it.

The pumps without prices. A coil of rope asleep in a flatbed. The slumbering trucks. Tinks was gassing the van up—"So what did you say this was, so late?"

David said, "My cousin," and took Tinks' cig away and puffed and heeled it out. "Not while you fuel."

Tinks clicked his tongue along with the clicking gallons.

"My cousin from Israel, he's coming to work for us. Tomorrow. Today. I'm setting up his house."

"Because there isn't any work in Israel?"

"Because there aren't any houses."

"He can't find anything for cheap in Palestine?"

"He just got out of the army."

Tinks rehung the nozzle. "Sounds gay."

"That's what they do: everyone in Israel goes into the army, and then when they get out, they go traveling."

"Everyone? Then who's left in Israel? Is Israel empty? Do the Muslim nations know this?"

"It's like to calm down, whatever."

"From what? From killing Arabs?"

"That's it, from killing Arabs."

"OK, I get it—even moving sounds calmer than that."

Tinks helped David load and when they finished David said, "You think you can help me stay awake out there?"

"Already?"

"I haven't asked you in a while."

"You haven't asked me since your coronary."

"You don't do that anymore?"

"I never did," but Tinks was already glooming over to his Dodge. He foraged in a compartment by the clutch and returned with a vial.

"I'll owe you," David said. "Put it on my tab."

Tinks said, "A parting tip from a pro?"

David snuffed from off the van key, "What?"

"You're going to want to cram your foam bumpers down into the wheelwells and mat the load so nothing frags."

The route was 440 through Bayonne—the emissions turbid in wind, the pollutants bracking the meadows. Past the natural gas plant's twinkling, the pressure vessels rose like foreign moons roiling with oil. This was what David relied on. This was what the city relied on: the terminals, the channels and trestles, the transmission substations, the transformers and pylons. The grid behind the grid, the truth that sustained the corruption. That's what David was always telling his daughter: without all this industry, the bistros would have to stop serving, the $6 latte stands would shut. No phones, no screens. No sweatshop thongs.

Staten Island was just a road between bridges and a drip that bittered his throat. The span heading in was so minor and hunched, the span heading out felt like a pompous suspension, multiple levels, multiple lanes. He always took the upper level, the waterward lane. He was in the midst of the bay, blowing his nose, when the sky exploded.

Streamers, fizzlers, snaps and pops. Enormous arteries of light rupturing the night, huge burst capillaries and veins. What was striking about fireworks was the expectancy involved. You were never sure if they were over. A rally would come, and the brilliance would spike, and then flatline away into vapors, and you'd tell yourself, that was it, that was the finale. But then there'd be a hiss, and you'd tell yourself, have patience, the ending is still coming.

In that way it was like getting old, or like waiting for dying.

The radio was airing some patriotic drumming and fife and bagpipe music but with a midtro rap, and David liked the beat, or he liked that he was familiar with the lyrics. He did another bump, vial to fingernail to the BQE. Then he took the necklace from his pocket and hung it from the rearview mirror, a sparkler never fading, just dangling, tinkling against the E-ZPass. He resisted the inclination to call his daughter.

He was sped up down Atlantic and making lights—past the bar where he'd last met her, which wasn't a cool bar, she'd said, but where sometimes she subbed, then past the bars where she usually worked, which got cooler, she'd said, the farther out they were, as the neighborhoods got worse—this last, of course, was his own opinion.

Some boys clattered by on bikes and threw firecrackers.

Tammy didn't like her father visiting her, especially not at her usuals. Where she served craft ales brewed with nutraceuticals and nanobatch liqueurs nextdoor to delis that had to post reminders about how foodstamps can't be used to buy diapers, tampons, sanitarypads, postagestamps, or any foods precooked.

In the mornings, she wrote. Because Tammy the bartender was also employed, underemployed, as a fundraiser, a grantwriter, by a nonprofit.

According to her, David's initial prejudice against her neighborhood was an insult, but an insult to her, because he tried to pass it off as concern. That was how he'd been raised. To be both racist and conceal it. To him, crime would always be going up and only statistics lived in Brooklyn. Crown Heights, Bedford-Stuyvesant. Their streets were just names on the news, associated with the city's youngest corpses. The boys crossing him at reds, provoking him by crossing his greens, staring him down. As if his color was the wrong color. But then every color was wrong if it was his. His color was Jewish, and yet even his daughter called herself a gentrifier, and the first time he'd heard that word, he'd heard it from her, it'd sounded British, fancy and goyish, like something she couldn't be, like something he couldn't be accused of having fathered. Strange that the word was masculine, though the predilections it indicated were feminine, or seemed feminine to him. Ladylike, dainty. She should say ladying instead. She should call herself a ladyfier. Back after she'd gotten sober, David had offered her the house he'd now be lending out to his cousin, to her cousin, but she'd refused. She'd only live in this neighborhood. All her friends lived here, so he'd bought here, from a Hasid related to a Hasid who'd owned the land under one of David's garages. A slumlord now hoping to offload his own brownstone and tow his bald wife and bawling kids upstate, to a secluded preserve of Talmud Torah. Tammy had the top two floors and rented out the garden apartment, which was a ladying or ladyfying euphemism for basement. The rent was hers to keep. David wasn't sure who was living there now. What charity case was getting a discount.

Still, it was turning out to be a solid investment—he had to admit, his daughter had pathologies, but she also had sechel. The neighborhood was improving. Each time he drove by, the dividingline had retreated by the block—with more cops out in cruisers, on hoof and foot, up cherrypicking in guardtowers— with more cafés, kindergartens, pet kindergartens, gyms. Her street had been sprucing by the house: with bricks repointed, stucco retouched, brownstone steamed.

He pulled around the corner, pulled up to the curb. The slits between the curtains were black. He grabbed the jewelry and, leaving the van running out of stimulant profligacy, ran up the stoop, lifted the mailbox top, pendulated the necklace over the slot and dropped it in. It made a whiny clink.

Queens—through the impassive park, David's heart beat fast and his breath fanned fast and sour. All around him was his youth. Where he'd taught Beth Shalom girls to tongue. Where he'd learned to roll joints and pound vodka stirred with Tang.

This was Flushing—or what still remained of it between Chinatown and Koreatown. Rezoned and redistributed, between one of the Chinatowns and one of the Koreatowns. On one of the dozens of wanton inordinate streets horning in between 37th and 46th Avenues. He checked his cousin's flight again, stopped just short of a rearending.

All those long noon days sitting on the floor and picking at the grouts, which wouldn't be picked at, because the tiles were just a print and the flooring was linoleum. All those longer nights his parents would be up arguing in the Yiddish of banged cabinets. This was the tacky tightwad pennycolored house his father went to work to get away from. Unlocking it meant bending the key, twisting so hard the key nearly broke and the vinyl-siding above the doorway sloughed its trim. This was the home his mother had cleaned and Ruth was supposed to have cleaned and now David had to scrub all the grease off himself. He'd never even touched a vacuum at his own residence.

Still, it wasn't the worst: the Bengali Bangladeshis, whose lease he'd guiltily terminated, and whose possessions he'd moved, for gratis, to a new condo in Forest Hills he'd found for them, for gratis—rather his employees had done all that for him and even tendered his regrets—hadn't left too many traces of their tenancy, just the lingering smell of an unplaceable spray or spice, something like a furniture polish of pepper and cinnamon. He examined the furniture, touched it for dust. It wasn't anything like what his parents had owned, but all that lot had been sold, or else had just gotten lumped in with all the other lots, in whichever warehouse, in whichever units. He wouldn't have recognized his parents' stuff anyway. He only recognized that his parents and his shift supervisor, under the influence of different Europes, had developed different tastes. Different deficiencies. Or maybe Jon had chosen this stuff. Or maybe Leland. His parents' modern would never be modern again. They'd gone for chrome, earth tones, rugs made of lla-mas. Not wood. Not such ponderous planking. Though some-thing about the diningroom table was familiar. Its dimensions or aridity, its chairs. Too many chairs. He swabbed at the stovetop, buffed the oven. Without a sponge, just with his hands, his fingernails, snorting rails off the table, snorting off a spoon. He stocked the cutlery drawer, decided his cousin could stock the pantry himself. Or else they'd stop together on the way back from the airport. At Stop & Shop. Or ShopRite. He climbed the mousy stairs.

It made sense that his parents' bedroom had been furnished. The only bed had been put in the largest bedroom, about as large as a closet should be, a cell for two immigrants to spend a life in, loving, hating, grappling. Jammed up against the sleigh bed were twin nightstands and an overdrawered dresser overdressed in carvings, oak clusters. Antiques, but that wasn't anything to recommend them. Dumpy, fusty, oppressively solid. Furnishings that prepared you for the coffin. Whoever had owned this stuff, whoever had stored and lost it, must be dead. David set his alarms, plugged in his phone, and went about laying the sheets, the fitted, the flat, the case for the pillow. "Fuck," which he pronounced aloud like a prayer before sleep, though he wasn't going to be able to sleep. That's what he'd forgotten: "Fucking pillows."

❋

Yoav, the dark kid, his cousin, his cousin's kid: only in that darkness would David ever recognize the boy already had a father.

The first time David met his cousin Yoav was 14 years before all this, when after 14 years of marriage his wife had caught him screwing, nailing, doing something industrious to an employee: doing some industry to Ruth.

David and Bonnie King, who was about to again become Bonnie Dhimmaj—a former calendar girl for a sportscar importer/exporter that David had longhaul dealings with—had been living in Jersey at the time, in a trophy mcmansion big enough for him to mope, her to rage, and their daughter to mourn in, but still: Bonnie threw him out, threw a garmentbag of suits to the porch. Jersey had been her dream, specifically the Jersey suburbs, specifically the suburb of Summit, the summit of success for the cityborn, and Bonnie was from the Bronx, an Eastern Orthodox who'd converted. David was facing a summer laid out in front of him like a scorched brittle lawn. He was facing a divorce and an attempt to invalidate the prenup. Bonnie would claim that her signature had been coerced, or forged, and regardless, he'd misreported assets. She'd also claim that he'd abused her and tried to get Tammy, bat mitzvah aged then, to back her up.

David moved into Manhattan but without his passport, considered breaking into the house to retrieve it on a day his accountant had told him that Bonnie was meeting with her own accountant, but then had reservations, took advice. He reported his passport as lost or stolen, applied to have a replacement expedited.

The day it arrived he went out and bought six of the same velcrotic insulated coolerbags, stopped by Citibank and dragged his suitcase into a cab to JFK, where he was met by Paul Gall and Pete Simonyi. He bought three roundtrip tickets and charged through the manifold security checks, hoping they might irradiate and change him.

The skin below his weddingband, where his weddingband had been, would tan.

Paul Gall, shift supervisor, was the most experienced, most decorated staffmember at King's Moving: back then, before the diabetes and arthritis, a big shambolic gorillalimbed guy with a widow's peak, a former mover's physique, and that egregious admiration for perceived Jewish business acumen so prevalent among the ex-Yugoslavs.

Pete Simonyi was David's lawyer: a small compact suit and tie guy with kinky hair and the solicitous airs of a minor advisor to a megalomaniacal regent.

For the flight to Tel Aviv, they sat toward the back of the plane, three in a three row with David lapsed insomniac in the middle through ten and a half hours, eight Nicorette lozenges, six Chivas Regals, and the disastrous mistaking of two pills of Fastin (the amphetamined weightloss supplement) for the identically colored, identically shaped, slowmaking, sleepmaking Ambien (generic Ambien)—meaning that he was always getting up and so making Paul Gall or Pete Simonyi get up and then sitting down again frenetic and tapping or shuffling his feet atop their carryons, which he'd had them shove under the seatrow in front.

He wouldn't, and wouldn't let anyone, stow them in the overheads.

There was a spate of blurry spy movies that'd been edited for sex and airborne violence, but David's English channel was broken, the dubbing was Hebrew, and the subtitles were Arabic, so he switched to a documentary about Israel.

David had first visited the country in the 1960s, when his father, who'd never been on a plane before, had flown the family over to be reunited with his younger brother, who'd been given up for dead in Poland. David returned solo in the 1970s, to pick citrus on a commie polyamory kibbutz, and then had tried taking Bonnie, from Paris, on their honeymoon, 1988 or so, just after the first bloom of the Intifada, but she'd refused.

"It wasn't the bombings that had her skittish," David said to his rowmates, "it was the hijackings, the planejackings."

He'd eaten the rolls off both neighboring trays and was now summoning a flightattendant for that transparent liquid she was pouring down the aisle: arak.

"I was going to take Tammy for her bat mitzvah, but Bonnie put the kibosh."

The flightattendant poured the arak into a cup and then, from a pitcher, added a sip of another transparent liquid, water, and his cup clouded over.

"There's nothing I don't regret."

El Al Flight 2 was expected to, but seldom did, arrive daily at Ben Gurion at 11:06 IDT. David sent his shift supervisor and lawyer to fetch his checked luggage, while he went to find a phone and find out how the phone worked and make a call.

He'd scrawled the number on a receipt he'd folded into his passport—to call Israel from within Israel he had to jettison the +00972: "Hello?"

A kid's voice picked up, in Hebrew.

"It's David King, hello? English? I'm calling for my cousin Dina. Put your mom on."

The kid hung up, so David tried again. He liked the long beeps, the long sheepish beeps, the phones in Israel rang with.

"It's me," he told Dina, once he got her. "Cousin David."

She said, "David," but like it wasn't Hebrew.

"I'm in Tel Aviv and free tomorrow if you're around."

The luggage was plunked in the trunk of the cab, but the carryons stayed on their laps—three men sitting scrunched again holding the insulated coolerbags with their shoeprints shifty all over them and pricetags still attached.

They rode through the insatiably bright Tel Aviv light that struck David like a divine obfuscation straight to the stark whitewashed cube that served as the international banking center of Bank Leumi.

They left the suitcases by a rindcolored bench under the watch of a hefty receptionist and followed a young guy who was friends or just colleagues with another young guy David had met all of a month ago at a stockbroker bar down on Pearl Street, to the rear of the bank and behind a flimsy felt partition, where they dumped the contents of the carryons: six bags,

$50,000 each, $300,000—the inaugural deposit of David's new account.

David was entrusting this money to Bank Leumi Israel with the explicit if unwritten understanding that if he'd ever have to access it, he'd just have to take a loan from Bank Leumi USA, essentially a sham loan to be collateralized in secret by the sum—by the tidy bundles of rubberbanded $100s—abiding innocently in Tel Aviv.

This arrangement—which was illegal and recommended by his lawyer—would allow David to deduct the interest paid on any loans as a legitimate business expense in the States, while his full intact sum earned taxfree interest abroad. Above all, though, this arrangement would allow him to keep considerable cash assets hidden from his wife, who was bent on taking him for everything, he was sure of it.

It was tough not to appreciate: the illegitimacy, the sleight, borrowing your own money, borrowing from yourself and never reporting it—David's future of meeting Israeli bankers in banyas and massageparlors in Manhattan to review the paperwork every quarter, because no statements would ever be sent through the mails.

The banker took the threesome out to lunch at a seaside fish restaurant and once the plates were all bones and the napkins wadded, he put in a call for a cab to take Pete Simonyi and Paul Gall back to Ben Gurion for the next return flight, whose duration would be just about equal to the amount of time they'd spent in Israel.

The lawyer had a trial and the shift supervisor had work too or was just daunted.

David's cab dropped the banker off at the bank (*bank*), and continued on through the citycenter (*mercaz ha'ir*) to the Dan Hotel (*malon Dan*), to an upgrade suite roughly the size and swankness of his new bachelorized apartment—but with a broad balconied view over the Mediterranean. The Mediterranean beats Central Park South.

This was David just daring himself, powering through, prodigalizing for confidence. He'd had enough of husbandly restraint. He was giving room to his native acquisitiveness. Four rooms with two full baths—everything here would validate his voracity.

The next morning, the second day—the day that God divided the sky from the waters below and so created the conditions for jetlag—David's cousins were waiting in the lobby: Dina and Yoav Matzav. There they were, standing—as if they didn't have the permission to do anything but stand—amid that zoo of Bauhausy loungery.

Dina Matzav was a nervous and yet, when she had to be, demonstratively hard woman, heavy at bottom, light in the waist and birdy above, and so she gave the impression of being both grounded and vulnerable, with that eggshell face still flawless but the hair even blacker than he'd remembered. She was the type who'd never dye her hair anything except the color it'd been when she was young, used makeup only to swear that she didn't, and moisturized furiously. She kept her clear manicure on her son's shoulders. Yoav was a skinny darkskinned kid like Aladdin from the Disney cartoon, six or seven years younger than Tammy, but scrawnier, taller, with that Maghrebi Jewish swarthiness, its stature and stretch. Between his mother and David, he stuck out, or was being stuck out, prodded into the heat of David's hug, which he accepted unwillingly and gawky, and David kissed his mother's cheek over his head. David had packed a moneybag with all the kidfriendly contents of his suite's minibar and welcomebasket—chocolate, pistachios, dried apricots and dates—and he presented it now like a gift for every belated occasion, and Yoav humped it out to the lot around the ficus and traffic bollards.

Along the way, Dina asked—she tried to ask—what brought David to Israel.

He said, "I figured we'd visit Jerusalem."

Dina's was a beaten red Renault and David was uncomfortable, both with how shoddy it was and how she was driving it. He sat up front and tried not to yank at the wheel. Yoav, in the clawed crumbstrewn rear, had gotten into the chocolate and was now bouncing a sticky smeared ball up against David's seatback and catching it, and then up against the back of David's headrest and catching it—until Dina yelled in Hebrew.

To David that defined Hebrew: the speech of the beleaguered, the last exasperation before a spanking.

She apologized—most of Dina's English was apology, mostly for her English, or for Yoav's behavior. The rest was all veterinary terminology and guidebook phrases that she'd repeat as if stalling, keeping her mouth limber until her mind had compromised between what she meant and an available expression.

Among her phrases were: "From time to time," "So nice," "That's incredible," and "The way it is." "From time to time" answered David's questions about how often she visited her father (whose name was Shoyl), and how often they used their air raid shelter because of rocket attacks (they lived in Bat Yam). "So nice" answered David's questions about how she liked living in Bat Yam and how Shoyl liked living in the senior home. "That's incredible" was Dina's response to David telling her about expanding his business into commuter Connecticut. "The way it is" was Dina's response to David telling her about his recent separation from his wife. David had said, "My shikse wife," despite Bonnie's conversion, and kept calling Dina's father by his Yiddish name, Shoyl, even while Dina stuck with the Hebrew, Sha'ul.

David talked through the hills, picking pet fur from his pants and twiddling the vents. As rubbleshouldered Route 1 rose into eyesquint and earpop, Dina had, or asked, just a single question: "We make the dinner after with Ilan?"

"Who's Ilan?"

"The husband of me. My husband."

Jerusalem, God's dwelling, overcharged for parking.

Dina huffed them up a ramp and through a ramparted gate into the Old City, only to slack and slow as if disoriented: she hadn't planned on anything beyond this point, she hadn't planned on having to do anything, beyond just picking up her cousin and bringing him here—that'd absorbed enough of her energies.

She'd just turned around and David had already bought Yoav a popsicle.

Anyway, it's not like there was anything to do but pray and shop. The Old City was just one continuous shop—a mall, but a stone mall, whose concourses were bound by stone and corrugated sheetmetal that kept the sun off.

"What you want to do?"

David wanted to sleep. To work. To have his daughter not

turned against him. To buy a hamsa keychain as a charm against death.

Yoav handed the popsicle to his mother and tarried by a table of souvenir shofars and icons and olivewood camels. He picked up a metal knot, two nails bent around each other.

David took it from him and solved the puzzle—aligning the nails and disentangling them: you had to bring them together to take them apart.

He put the pieces in Yoav's palm, and Yoav held his gaze with awe.

Yoav was trying to tangle them up again, but Dina took the pieces away and left them on the table.

David was down the street, trying to find that café he'd once liked. Where he'd gotten drunk on slivovitz with those Dutch blonde girls with whom he'd harvested oranges. Where he'd gotten silly high with those Dutch blonde girls as firm and smooth as oranges. He was trying to remember that one café that'd spiked its hookahs with opium.

"Remember the winter I was here?" he asked. "76 or 77?"

Dina handed him the popsicle. "Not very."

She'd been too much a child then, too related to him to be interested.

The younger David would've climbed the citadel of David, but the ticketbooth was closed now and he was older and worried about lacking the lungs for it.

"What year was King David?" he asked. "What century? He was before zero, I know. Before Jesus."

Dina replied what she replied: "So nice," "That's incredible."

That's how it went: with David putting questions to Dina

about the sites—about the Sepulchre church atop where Jesus was buried? or atop where Jesus was crucified? which was built during which of the Crusades? and how many Crusades were there, anyway? Not that he was asking for a tour, not that he'd ever admit he was asking, but only because he enjoyed his cousin's bewilderment, he enjoyed—the few times she ventured to answer—cutting her off and correcting: "There definitely weren't seven Crusades, I'm thinking the number's like five."

An order of nuns was crossing the Via Dolorosa and, while David went elbowing through, Dina stepped into an alley, tugging Yoav by the collar and muttering a remark that her son picked up like a shiny shekel from the gutter. He laughed. He wouldn't stop repeating it. A rough translation would be: "There were seven Crusades, you rabid asshole"—and a scraggly Armenian priest streaking by stiffened and winced and the Palestinians outside their shops leaning against their flipflop racks grinned.

The stones now increased in size, until the individual blocks seemed to outgrow their cuts and became pure stone itself, the surfaced substance of the earth through which the narrowing corridors had been quarried. Yoav quieted. He walked by David's side, then walked slower, behind him, with Dina coming last. They were being pressured, singlefiled, lined.

The Hasid just ahead of them put his book into a bin, which he nudged down the conveyor to get xrayed, but the French just ahead of the Hasid kept setting off the metal detectors and so were returned again through the gantries to remove their belts. A Scandinavian woman plumped by middleage and with hair like a wilted palmtree was trying to banish the ecstasy from her face while being patted down.

That was it, David realized, as he helped Yoav on the steps—as he helped Yoav leap between the steps—Jerusalem wasn't a mall, its walls only contained a mall, because given all its gates and security checkpoints, it was more like another airport. A mystical airport. A ruined terminal connecting future and past. More than international, interstellar. And there lording it over the wide thronged plaza was the board. But instead of listing the Arrivals and Departures, the Kotel, the Western Wall, was cracked and brown and blank. Travelers kept glancing up at it, as if expecting the announcement of a delay. They scrambled to keep up with their groups: Japanese with the Japanese, Georgians and Russians with the Russians, Australians and Canadians with the British, everyone hustling toward their linguistically appropriate flags, which were held aloft by guides who shrieked through megaphones, distorting histories.

David helped himself from a trough of flimsy nylon yarmulkes, palmed one onto Yoav—"We boys will meet you here," he said, and steered Yoav to the line to the left, to the men's prayer area, and Dina shrugged, but instead of joining the line to the right, to the women's, she stepped back from the corrals to make a phonecall.

The stones were beset by men swaying, jostling, shuckling, bowing from the waist, wrapped up in tallis and tefillin. It was all uniform, or all about the uniform, the heavy gabardines of the European ghettos interlayered with modern weatherproofed fatigues, and it was this semblance, this belonging, which inverted the usual fashion dynamic and made the secular

39

civilian visitors seem suspicious, out of place: the religious were in charge here, and the soldiers were too, and everyone else was a tourist, garbed in tshirts, shorts, and shame, lotioned up, in visors.

David bowed his head. He inclined himself toward concentration, as if the lower his head, the better his chances of remembering, because memory was deep. His face up against the stones, he tried to summon psalms, but all that came to mind was whether his co-op would approve a dog, and if so, of what size. Ruth knew he wasn't going to marry her, because of which, he knew, she wasn't going to quit and he wasn't going to fire her, which would mean getting hit for wrongful termination atop harassment. Maybe he'd adopt a feral tabby, maybe a passive aggressive Abyssinian bred by a colleague of Dina's. Or else he'd just get an aquarium. Or like a greenhouse but for lizards. His brain wasn't wired for prayer, just panic. He hadn't spoken to his God since Bonnie had gone into labor with Tammy.

Bonnie, the Fordham Road Albanian Orthodox who'd dipped in the mikveh and stepped out dripping for him—so as to always have leverage on him—had been the one who'd gone to shul, while David had shown up begrudgingly only twice a year, thrice this past year if he counted Tammy's bat mitzvah, to which he'd invited his office manager.

Bonnie had been livid—the goal was to cut down the guestlist, the affair was already getting out of control—but David had prevailed.

He was inviting his foremen, his facility chiefs—why not his office manager? Wasn't Ruth the employee he worked the closest with?

She wouldn't be allowed to bring a date, she'd be seated with Tammy's old babysitters. Peace had to be maintained among the staff.

It was a week or two after that everything collapsed. Bonnie knew it all. He still didn't know whether Bonnie had followed them herself or had paid to have them followed. Romantic Bayonne: sirloins at the Broadway Diner and noodles and Guinness at Thai O'Brien's, because Ruth wasn't the type you had to bring into the city.

David confessed, he had to, and what Bonnie blurted out would remain her grievance, or the only grievance she ever aired in front of Tammy: "You invited that bitch to the bat mitzvah, where you danced with her."

She'd burned with incredulity: "That's when I knew, when you danced with that Jew bitch, in front of all our friends and family."

All this came back to David at the Wall, and he was crying, and a child's hand squeezed his.

"What?" he said. "Everything's OK."

Yoav tugged—his face, upturned, had the anonymous expectancy of an entire audience in it, an entire congregation: well-wishing but impatient, under a thicket of curls and a dimpled yarmulke. David had invited his office manager to the bat mitzvah, but not his cousins.

"What's going on, bud?"

Whatever Yoav was saying teemed with urgency. He was also grabbing his crotch.

"Bathroom—you have to go to the bathroom? Fuck. OK. Number one or number two?"

Yoav picked at his zipper.

"Can you ask someone? I mean, where—I don't know where—I'm sorry, I don't know Hebrew. Lo speak ivrit, OK? I'll find someone, and you'll just ask them."

It had to be down by the plaza's edge: shitting and pissing were definitely prohibited in such close proximity to the most sacred.

They waited their turn—"You can do this on your own?"

Huddled in the stall, David was relieved that his cousin stood. When Yoav was finished, David kicked out a loafer and flushed the toilet with his foot—"Keeps your hands clean," he said, and Yoav's smile had understanding.

Coming back from the WC complex to the meetingpoint, Dina wasn't there.

David surveyed the crowd and then circled around and checked the lines: for the women's WCs, they were eternal.

"Let's go up to the Mount," he said. He took off his yarmulke, and then Yoav's, crumpled them in a fist—"the Temple Mount, what do you say, bud?"

They had to pass through another checkpoint: Yoav slipped through, but David was made to stand to the side as a wand was waved over him, as if in a rite of purification.

The ascent was steep, up a sort of scaffolded gangway, a provisional span of juryrigged piping and plywood, to the platform above the Wall, and of which the Wall was but the western retainer—the Kotel being structural, loadbearing, which means the Muslims can never move it, all their mosques would fall.

David took Yoav around the mosques like they owned them, or were inspecting them, preparing estimates on properties they'd have to haul out—stripping the smaller dome of its leaded silver, stripping the bigger dome of its low karat gold, and then clearing them both of all the rugs and lanterns and loudspeakers inside, all the ewers and lavers and shoes removed by worshippers, and even that pocked lunar rock, where the altar of the temple used to be, where the ten commandments, the holy stone tablets, used to be: the ark of the covenant had been a box—should've been easy to port, easy to store, two Puerto Ricans could've handled it.

A man blocked the way—"No to visit"—and other men rose from their feetwashing in the vestibule and gathered behind him and David hugged Yoav close just as the man spit and the gob of phlegm landed on the cuff of David's pants. Men massed toward them, beckoning, yelling, with only one of them coherent, "I am sorrow for all this," he said, and though the others were only yelling at the one who'd spit, David didn't notice, he just turned, lifted Yoav up in his arms and quickened his steps and as the Arabic faded another thing flew—not a rock, not even a pebble, just like a clod of fertilized dirt whizzed through the air between their heads, hit the ground ahead of them and scattered toward the scandalously baretrunked trees at platform's ledge, as David shielded Yoav, and heaved them both toward the exit.

Yoav was in tears and David didn't recognize the streets.

"Hey bud, hey, it's alright."

The street was lined with nuts and sesame seeds and vendors curious.

"It's alright, calm down. Everything's fine, bud."

But Yoav wouldn't hush until David had bought him the exact same metal knot from a different stand that sold the exact same things.

Coming around to the descent to the plaza again, they had to pass through the security checkpoint again, and the nails set off the detector, and as David was trying to explain to the guards what a puzzle was, Dina rushed up shaking admonishment with her phone—"To where you go?"

"We weren't sure where you were."

Dina snapped at the guards, exited the wrong way and tossed herself onto her son. "I make the phonecall with the patient who have the parrot that do not talking."

"We went up to the Temple Mount."

Dina bit a lip and then asked Yoav, who confirmed for her in Hebrew, and then she said to David, "You can not."

"We did."

"You can not to go, it not safe. The warning he is there to say that, we forbidden."

"We?"

But she, who was frantic, meant only Yoav—because with Americans, who cared? Did it ever matter what they violated?

"Anyway," David said, "what causes a parrot to lose its speech? Does it forget what it regularly says or just lose its vocal ability completely?"

All the ride back Dina was silent and fuming.

They passed a sign for Ben Gurion—in Israel, it felt like you were always going to, or from, or merely passing the airport, and every sign told you how far you were from the airport, as if it were important to be constantly aware of the precise kilometer distance between this life and an escape.

At the Tel Aviv limits, they left Route 1 for Bat Yam.

Dina's house formed one wall of a dusky courtyard: a clumpy sandbox litterbox, a swingset without swings, a slide without a ladder, and a seesaw jutting up from the weeds like an errant missile. The unit itself was groundfloor and underventilated, a lair of wetsplotched drywall and lumpy carpet, where Dina's husband, Ilan Matzav—a stocky man with resentful muscles and sparse facial hair, a nativeborn Israeli who resembled Arafat—sat detached and spraddled macho atop a Genuine Leather Couch, whose ruff had a label that read Genuine Leather Couch, surrounded by hairball and shed and two cute aloof girls somewhere between Tammy's age and Yoav's: tawny cousins from the Matzav side, who resided in the opposite unit. There was a palsied dog in a cage that David assumed was named Shollie, but that turned out to be the breed, German shepherd/border collie, and its name instead was Simba. There were cats too, stippled mixes swingdooring in and out of the house, and a fuzzy Siberian without a tail that the girls passed between their laps and might've called Shirazi. Yoav was sitting crosslegged atop the maybe leather maybe not ottoman of his father's maybe leather maybe not clubchair, which had been surrendered—in an unrecognized, at least unappreciated, surrender—to David. Yoav's grandmother, Ilan's mother, Safta Sara, whiskered in sniffing warily—it was like she'd just managed to sneak out of the kitchen alive and with this tray of bourekas she offered around, but wouldn't let go of, she wouldn't put it down, she wouldn't sit down. Dina was in the kitchen, chopping salads, chopping—because David was in the midst of retelling what'd happened, but now lightly, as if he were telling a joke, because the anecdote had already become, like the round mosaic table, patterned, stylized. He kept prodding with his loafer at Yoav's ottoman, prodding anxiously at the kid to agree, but Yoav was too transfixed by the spit dried on David's pantscuff and Simba barked until brought to heel by Ilan with a green bone treat.

Ilan's English was decent—or just familiar to his cousin by marriage—because though he was now a master welder responsible for the lines at the Ashdod refinery that attached to the Eilat-Ashkelon Pipeline, his previous jobs had taken him to rigs and platforms all over the world, whose guttural lingua franca was Fucking Shit: "Fucking Arabushim," he said, and pointed at a chromeframed photo on the wall of who he said was his only brother Shachar who'd died in Lebanon, "Shit the brain Arabushim," and Dina called out from the kitchen something in Hebrew as thick and gristly as her lamb tajine, gulped down with lukewarm Schweppes.

After, the whole family accompanied David to the door. Even Safta Sara who, each time she waved, put her hand to the mezuzah, then to her lips. The girl cousins rowdied around in the yard chasing beetles. Yoav tried to follow Dina and David to the car, but Ilan held him back, held him as he squirmed, and night beat its wing over his farewell: "Byegoodbye."

A hypermarket, a pharmacy, a dun huttish structure topped with a blinking red neon star that didn't mean synagogue but ambulance dispatch—Dina was wrenching the Renault around the roundabouts, taking grim turns at sharp angles.

A crumbling aggregate of residential buildings quaked up on rickety struts as if they were about to falter on prostheses. She parked beneath them and across two spaces, leaned her head against the wheel and said, "Infection of bacteria or fungus, but if she losing the feathers also then maybe parasite or herpes, or maybe only that a feed pellet she is eating is sticking. That is how the parrot she is losing the voice."

"So it doesn't have to do with memory?" David said.

"Tomorrow," she said, "it more better to make the visit tomorrow. To make prepare for him."

"But I fly back in the morning," David insisted and Dina sighed and offed the engine.

"Thanks," he said. "Todah rabah. Been meaning to say, that son of yours is a good smart kid. Didn't want to forget that."

A bell had to be pressed, and the door buzzed like locusts into a utilitarian lobby lined with padded railings, tacked agendas flapping blank and, toward the back, under the missing panels of the dropceiling, a librarianlike attendant in a smock, with hair and makeup seared the purple of a sweet Carmel wine, and on her chin a lesion shaped like Ukraine.

Dina, after pleasantries that weren't returned, translated her gist for David almost triumphantly: "She say to me that we too late."

The attendant, not to be shown up, reverted to that language: "It is no more the hours of visiting."

"But he's her father," David said. "He's my father's brother and in the morning I fly."

The attendant opened her crossword book, but turned away. David, like he was marking her page, laid down the rest of his shekels.

Dina summoned the elevator. The moon of wired plexiglas lit.

The topfloor hall reeked of bleach. All toilets handicapped, a rollingcart slavered with babywipes, rummikub tiles, and novels in Hebrew, English, the Cyrillics, and what was either Arabic or Persian. A scrum of IV stanchions. A gurney.

Namecards marked the doors, and theirs was at the end. Dina knocked, but it was unlocked, it didn't have a lock, and she entered knocking, into a room the size of a cell in solitary. A cubby held folded tracksuits, a pill slicer, pills. Some device, which might've served some pulmonary function, was off, and so now was just the expensive medical pedestal for a boombox. The man appeared to be nude, besides the artbook covering his sex splayed wide to a doublepage spread that reproduced another nude, lusher and Flemish, and the immense headphones clamped to his bulbous baldness that leaked a string music, soaring, jarring, Viennese. He sat on a backless aluminum stool, his scabbed shins straddling a quadcane wrapped with electrical tape like a sticky black mummy. His skin was sheetwhite, his gut untucked and stitched with scars and parchmentcolored patches. And there, on his forearm, was his camp number, its zeroes smudged.

Dina brought her face close to her father's and touched his temples, and the man startled up, but timidly, and she lifted the headphones off and removed the book, under which he was wearing just a faded figleaf of diaper.

David said, "Shalom, Uncle Shoyl—it's Yudy's son, David," but the man just sat there and Dina stood smug. "It may be for him that he is not now knowing English," she said to David and then, "Aba, Aba, English, Anglit—yes no hello?"

Still the man didn't stir and Dina shrugged, "The way it is from time to time."

"Yudy, your brother? He was my father, my tate. I'm David, you understand—you farshteyn? The last I visited you I was young—a hippie, a schlep. I'd come to Israel running away from the business. Running away from Dad."

The man seemed to be clearing a nest from his throat and David turned to Dina, who raised her palms, "He forget also Yiddish, I thinking. You tell me."

David tried again, "From Vrbau, you remember?"

Vrbau, or Verbó, or Vrbové, was the town in Austro-Hungary, then later in Czechoslovakia, where it all began: the nativity of David's father Yudy and his younger brother, Shoyl, who now cocked his head at David and said, "This is the BBC."

"Who?"

"This is London calling."

Yudy and Shoyl were the only members of the Klinger family to survive the Hlinka Guard and the Nazi SS. In summer 1942 they were deported to the Sered transit and labor camp, in summer 1944 Yudy was sent to Theresienstadt and then, because he'd become a skilled mason, to Buchenwald, while Shoyl, who was underweight and tubercular, was sent to Auschwitz. After Liberation, Yudy married a woman from the DP pens and went to meet the remnant of her family, who'd made it to the States. In New York, he Americanized his name to Jay King and worked as a driver for a freight agency, until he'd saved up enough to buy his own truck, to fix it up, then a legion of trucks, bought marshland and threw up a garage, established a moving concern.

His brother, Shoyl, the man sitting there while David fed him his memories, staggered around Europe until he reached Trieste, from which he smuggled himself by boat to Corfu, and then to Jaffa in what was Palestine, Hebraicized his name to Sha'ul Ben Kinor, joined the Palmach, distinguished himself fighting both the British and Arabs, and sometime after the founding of Israel married a Polish survivor whose family was setting up a grocery. The brothers got back in touch in the 60s, through a Vrbové newsletter.

Sha'ul, David's uncle, would only say: "Yudy—Yehudah—he went to America," and though David encouraged him, all the man would say after was, "He is working as mechanic, with oil on his hands, because he is not educated," which referred, it seemed, because Dina was grumbling, to Dina's husband, Ilan.

Sha'ul said, "Mizrahi. This means Sephardi, Arab Jew, but he is more like Arab, not Jew. If Mizrahim are being religious they stupid and if not being religious more stupid. Because the religion is all they have."

David was nearly yelling, "I'm Yudy's son, David. From America. From New York. Visiting you in Israel. Today we went to Jerusalem. You ever go up on top of the Wall—the Temple Mount?"

Dina grunted, as David retold again what'd happened until Sha'ul's face wandered to a leak in the ceiling.

"The last time," he said and David stopped and Sha'ul assembled his breath, "the last time I go up to Jerusalem was 1948 when I liberate it."

✻

And that was it, that was everything. David wasn't in contact with the family again, not until recently: they didn't come to the States, he didn't go there. No rendezvous, no nothing. That visit of his had been so brief and the intervening drift so tolltaking and straining that in retrospect it all seemed to him like an airplane dream—a dream so narcotized and fitful that he could barely remember it, or could give only the broadest synopsis. If since his return David had paid any mind to his cousins at all, it was only when he was reminded of their state—when he had his quarterly conclaves with his bankers, when he found himself stopping in Fair Lawn, Tenafly, or Paramus, to dine at some overlit abattoirish joint with an out of date map from the Bible tacked between the falafel fryer and the spit of incognizable frozen shawarma, or when some Palestinian incursion or Israeli reprisal had fared so spectacularly as to flare up on primetime or the talkradio news. And though he worried, of course, because he always worried, he was also lazy, selfish, and busy, so that his thoughts regarding Israel tended to be similar to his thoughts regarding crises among his vendors and suppliers: namely, that his own core business was strong, moving and storage would always be strong, and that if any of the suffering ventures he dealt with—which supplied him, say, boxes, crates, and fuel—hadn't implemented sufficient systems and management protocols, then that was their problem, not his, and should he ever get involved and try to solve anything—should he do anything beyond just holding an opinion, or having a wish, or expressing a desire—he'd only succeed at making a fool of himself, making trouble.

In other words: there wasn't nothing he could do.

Of course, just because David wasn't in contact didn't mean the Israelis didn't try.

They'd tried twice—or Dina had—by email.

The first email had arrived in the fall, just after David's return, when the Twin Towers went down—Dina was checking up on him, with a barrage of grief tinged only slightly with the gloating suggestion that now New Yorkers were experiencing what Israelis were already, immemorially, accustomed to.

The second email had arrived the fall after that, when Shoyl, or Sha'ul, died of pneumonia, and David had at least read that one, and intended to reply.

But it'd been a difficult time. He'd been busy.

He'd had his own, his immediate, family to tend to—their immediate splinterings. His divorce.

His wife—who was holding out for a sum she refused to specify before she agreed to become his exwife—Bonnie, was a disaster. She was accusing him of tight fists, closed fists, and sexually assaulting her while under the influence of cocaine, Ambien, and Lunesta. She had a group of cleanshaven hunky trainee priests representing the Albanian Diocese of the Autocephalous Eastern Orthodox Church show up at the Jersey office to deliver a massive, impressively calligraphed scroll annulling her conversion, and then not content with that, she took out a fullpage announcement to that same effect in *The Jersey Journal* and *Star-Ledger*.

Ruth left her Chrysler outside Bill Jr's school and returned from a conference with the viceprincipal to find its doors all keyed up and a hotpink swastika spraypainted, but spraypainted backward, across its hood, an act of vandalism that David insisted—though he wasn't convinced and Ruth wasn't either—was a coincidence.

After the settlement, after Bonnie's lawyer got frustrated and forced her to settle, it's not like life improved.

Because Bonnie was poisoning their daughter against him and indulging her, completely. She'd given her the run of the Summit house, letting her have parties, poolparties, letting boys stay over, jacuzzi boys, and so Tammy floated through highschool high and drunk and popular and if she hadn't tested so well, or excited such enthusiastic recommendations out of her male instructors, she'd never have gotten into college. The only college she applied to: NYU.

Though it's not like New York brought Tammy closer to her father—the fact that he was paying full tuition, and full incidentals, was responsible for that, not to mention that the moment she was out of Summit, Bonnie listed the house, sold it fast and cheap and left for Las Vegas, where a guy who'd customized the Porsches she used to model on had opened a strictly American rodder shop and did a decent trade.

David remembered the guy from around the Port—he was, himself, like a domestic vehicle: amiable, reliable, lunkish.

2007: Tammy was in touch with David only if she'd depleted

her monthly allowance and needed cash and so she was in touch with him every month. David would invite her up to Central Park South, but she wouldn't go, though neither did she want him Downtown, where they might bump into one of her student friends who all majored in communications but minored in avoiding interactions with parents, or into one of the men roughly David's age she'd been hanging around with—the men single, separated, cheating—who, if they weren't themselves lining up to give Tammy the extra money, then were at least buying her the substances she was otherwise trying to get the money for, or buying her drinks and dinners. The result of this geographic impasse was the declaration of a swath of no man's land for their father/daughter meetings: that territory north of 14th Street along Broadway, which careered through its intersections in an abrupt greenlined curve like an addict tweaked and reeling—a strip, as opposed to a proper neighborhood, notable only for having the world's highest per capita concentration of ATMs.

The amounts Tammy asked for kept increasing and she asked with an increasing shrilling frequency and David— hearing out her justifications on a pedestrian refuge—told her to stop going clubbing so much and to take more advantage of her mealplan and dorm: she looked thin and underslept.

She, so unlike her father, was into going slow. Heroin. But snorted not shot. That was what she'd tell the hallmates she'd initiated: "I snort it, never shoot it." That was what she'd tell herself, when she left the hall for her dealer's apartment on Delancey: "Nostrils, not needles." She also dabbled in anorexia and bulimia, her head like a brunette plunger in the toilet. Her grades went south. Downtown as south as Wall Street, where the better dealers operated out of cubicles and dressed with all the natty neatness of hedgefunders but behaved with all the volatility of the market. She'd nod off at the Battery. Or on the ferry. Or else in a cab on the way to some rave boroughed past all consciousness and when she came to again she'd have to talk herself, or do something more degrading than talk herself, out of the fare. One upside of having a drug habit is that you pick up a bit of Spanish. Which, as a sophomore, was the only class she wasn't failing, Spanish II. That summer, she told her father she needed cash to go to California to do some organizing of Mexican farmworkers. She needed some volunteership to put on her resume, though she'd already had ample experience with illegal and/or temporary labor, in which she'd developed her skills at bargaining, dissembling, arbitrage, and fraud. David refused, because he was stingy, but also because he was dubious, so Tammy got a Dominican friend from Summit, who was lately a frat brother at Rutgers, to set up a bilingual website for the farmworker seminar and the money appeared—it had to appear—David had Ruth cut a check and mail it c/o Rutgers. The cashed sum, or most of it, made it to Tammy, who turned it over to a Fujianese who didn't own, but who purported to own, a raw but still expensive floorthrough loft on Kenmare, where Tammy settled in with two NYU philosophers and the dregs of Delta Kappa Epsilon of New Brunswick. That summer was mostly a drought, though: the Wall Street connections left to supply out of town, which just might've been an idiom for jail, and it got to the point that some hapless fratters had re-gressed to skulking through Washington Square and mugging for the cameras, while others had finally succumbed to the sharps, shooting product that threatened coma.

After not getting through to Tammy in almost two months, David called Bonnie. He'd figured, given California, Tammy might've visited her mother in Nevada.

But Bonnie hadn't talked to their daughter either and had no information about interning at farms.

David called the bank, which just told him his check had been cashed. The seminar's website was down. He told Tinks to keep reloading. He pressed redial like a tremor. He was haunting the NYU library, trying to find her friends. He'd importune anyone likely. Because of shortness of shorts, because of waif insouciance of tanktop. Smokers.

He didn't know how else to seek her out—the school registrar wouldn't tell him who her dormmates were.

A guy leaving the library bummed a cig. He didn't know Tammy, but guessed which classes she'd taken. David called the professors at home, but none remembered her. Bonnie phoned to say she'd seen their daughter in Vegas. She'd been driving down the Strip and seen her. Tammy had been riding an escalator, up—she'd had a baby.

But then Bonnie's new husband was on the line—"Carl here, Bonnie-lass has been drinking."

"Is that it?"

"Margaritas," the new husband said as, behind him, Bonnie squawked. "You'll keep us in the loop, please, David?"

"I will, Carl."

"It's tough."

"It has to be," David said. "Any other way, it wouldn't feel like living."

A week later, Tammy met a pearly Ford Taurus at that square where Centre becomes Lafayette and as she climbed out of the back clutching her powder, not in glassine as usual, but folded jankily in unscratched lottery scratchers, the car was swarmed by cops.

David bailed her out and had Pete Simonyi find her a lawyer, who got her released into rehab to be followed by 100 hours of community service and so she'd get her volunteer experience after all.

David had Ruth drive him in her Chrysler to and from the rehab facility in the Catskills. He needed her chattering, he needed her turnsignaling, that steady click.

She kept him patient. She suggested they walk and so they walked, around the facility's grounds, on trips during which Tammy had turned them away: needle trees dulled with snow and an iced stream trickling into an offproperty cataract. This was the closest Ruth had ever come to snaring David in a couple: winter weekends strolling between surveilled stands of pine, trying not to lose the trail, until the trail hit a perimeter wall and they'd aboutface.

Then it was spring, 2008: the worst year not to own your whole home in America, the best year to own an American moving business.

And Tammy was thawing—one week she traipsed out to the gate and stood in the rain talking to David while Ruth sat in the car.

"You're looking good," he said. "Putting on pounds."

"Mom's been sending packages."

"Good."

"She sent me a scarf and candy eggs this time. She's getting weirder."

"She's your mother."

"I take after her, she says."

"She thinks it's all my fault."

"What about her?" Tammy gestured toward Ruth in the car. "What does she think—or is she not allowed to?"

Ruth gave a cautious wave back.

"Hear me out, Tam—I'm your father," and he held his umbrella out between them, so that neither was sheltered. "My father, you know I don't talk about him much, but the camps fucked him up. He had so many expectations, so many ambitions, all this anger. And this is where we are now."

"Standing in the fucking rain talking about the Holocaust?"

"This is where we are," David said. "So when I became a father, because things were better for me, all I had to be was better than he was. And I tried to be. I tried to give you everything."

"And now you feel bad about it."

"It was the only way I knew how," he said, and brushed his sopping coat.

"We all have our excuses."

The next week, Tammy communicated through the rehab facility's counseling office: David, and Ruth if she must, was to be admitted up to the bungalow.

She'd made grilledcheese, Tammy had, skillet on a hotplate. She poured out a single seltzer among them, lit up and went outside.

Tammy was smoking constantly and David joined her but only for every second cigarette, father and daughter bundled in the doorway under the overhang, butts collecting in the hollows of the drainage mat below. The cigarettes that David skipped he stayed inside with Ruth, who was cold to him, because she was being left alone and he was oversmoking and he reacted to that treatment by being obnoxious himself, by ignoring her—because she'd made him leave his thermos of rye in the trunk.

The moment they were finished and headed for the city, David planned to unscrew the lid and drink—he had just enough left to drink himself out of the woods, but not enough to get through the Bronx.

The bungalow was a warren of rooms around a common room—four other recoverers lodged there and because it was never not raining, they were in the same common room too, or in and out of it. The TV was always on, because it gave everyone—stranger residents, stranger adults—something to talk about or not. Everything the screen showed, it greened, as if underwater, or behind a static cloud. Coming back from a cig, David found one of the residents sitting in his place on the sofa next to Ruth and so now sitting between him and Ruth—she was a retard, which term Ruth would disapprove of in the car, but which David would insist on, because Tammy insisted, the girl had been normal before the drugs, she'd had every advantage including the drugs and her brain had come to this: tomato methadone soup. She was clamoring for some sitcom and Tammy didn't respond and was telling David not to, but the retard kept yowling, until Ruth got up—there was no remote— and switched the channel. A gameshow turned to news, but before Ruth had realized and dialed higher, David said, "Don't," and he smiled at the retard, who mouthed, "Thank you," and settled against a cushion contented.

Onscreen was the sky, blue like a foreign sea, bottomed with scrolling sports scores. Rockets were skimming through the distance. Skimming so evenly, so peacefully, and the sky was peaceful too. They came in graceful arcs. In elegant convexities. The effect was oddly lulling. It was only when the shot swooped in, when it zoomed in, that there was any sense of spiral, of a slight tight spiraling anxiousness, like how sperm wriggle up toward the solar egg, and then the anchor broke in with commentary about the unprecedented profusion of new Grad missiles—made in Russia, obtained from Iran—being shot into Israel from Gaza.

David, as if he didn't have to explain himself, said, "I wonder how they're doing."

Tammy said, "Who?"

"Your cousins."

"Who cares?"

Ruth still stood alongside the set, awkwardly canted toward it like she was demonstrating its features on the shopping network.

After a moment, David said, "I care. Tell me you're not subscribing to that bullshit."

Tammy said, "It's a criminal regime."

David said, "Who's a criminal regime? The Palestinians? The Saudis? The NYPD, or the dopedealers they got off your block?"

"Israel, Dad. Fatah, Hamas, Hezbollah—they're all just fighting for their freedom, for Palestinian freedom, and Israel's the rogue state at this point."

"This is what you learned at NYU?"

"What I learned at NYU was just how psycho Jews are. Every protest against Israel, half the people protesting are Jews."

"Self-hating, self-antisemites. Or else they're just being slaves to the trends."

"No: they just realize how fucked up it is, to have this country across the ocean that claims to be their home and defend them, that murders in their name."

"You're serious, Tam?"

"Or else the rallies are just for political bros to meet women. To try and fuck women. Divest, boycott. Enough with the torture, let's bone."

"Defending Jews—that's not a valid stance for a Jewish country, given history?"

"I don't think so, Dad. Sincerely."

"You're not worried that you have family impacted?"

"Whose family? Does this family I've never met worry about me?"

"Worry about what, Tam?"

"Anything. How we treat our own minorities. What you do for a living, dispossessing. What I'm going through here, my recovery."

"At least in America, you lose your house, you can get it back from the bank. In Israel, you lose it to the rockets."

"People my age, they're just tired of everything, or of having to care about everything. Lobbyists. The money they make. The killing."

"You're not making sense—you're conflating. Ruthie, will you back me up?"

Ruth, cripped over, said, "About Israel? I've never been. I'd prefer Cancun, if anyone would ever take me. But frankly, I'm happy in Hoboken."

Tammy said, "Or else it's like an addiction. Politics is, or how you feel about what you are is, or how you feel about identity and what it makes you do. Same appetite. It all depends on what you like: uppers or downers."

But David was still tuned to Ruth. He said, "Cancun and Hoboken, the promised lands."

Tammy said, "It's all just a matter of being exhausted with whatever's your normal. Over there, the Palestinians launch rockets and become suicide bombers—over here we just OD."

David said, "You're talking at me, over me. Conflating."

"You don't listen, you don't see what's in front of you, you're living in another world," Tammy said. "Turn it off."

The next day, David set a meeting with his local Bank Leumi banker—not his regular guy, who'd been called back to Israel for reserve duty, but a new guy—over secondfloor Bukharan in the Diamond District: plov and kettled tea.

David went into the meeting proposing to take out a loan on all the lode he still had stowed there, but was ultimately persuaded against it—because the rockets didn't always lead to war, and if they did, the war was always quick.

He left the meeting pledging to deposit even more cash, significantly more, into his Israeli account—that is, if he wouldn't have to transport it himself again, physically.

He left the meeting with a feeling of victory.

Tammy earned her sobriety certificate, returned to school, to the dorms, completed her community service spiking trash in Union Square, did her semester abroad in Prague, and on her way to visiting Budapest stopped in Vrbové.

She aced all her tests and her drug tests, was graduated from

NYU, and as a present David bought her that brownstone in Crown Heights.

She got a smattering of writing assignments and published a report on rape and New York bar culture, others about frisking policy and profiling by cops, but it was her series defending the success rates of Vodou drug therapies among New York's Haitian population—against legal challenges seeking to criminalize the act of transferring a crack addiction to a goat, which was then butchered—that precipitated an offer from the developmental assistance and humanitarian relief NGO, which meant that she wasn't going to come work for her father anytime soon.

And then just before Passover, this spring, 2015, David had a numbness, then a lancination in his chest—while making the turn from the Belt Parkway to the BQE on his way back from a sheriff's office vs. marshal's office charity touch football game. It was a heartattack so mild he'd driven himself to the hospital.

And not the nearest hospital, but Mount Sinai.

The situation wasn't remotely lethal, just unnerving. Bedbound, the hardest thing had been managing Ruth, her nurture and advances.

In the depths of his convalescence, which lasted all of half a month, he'd received an email, from his cousin Dina, the Subject: of which was vaguely ominous:

Re: Bad New, it read, and given the linguistic barrier he could only guess that the intention had been *Bad News*, though that *Re:* was somewhat reassuring, in that it meant that his cousin hadn't developed any telepathic powers but rather marked the communication as a continuance of something preexisting, of an earlier chain being summarily exhumed, resurrected, and rattled. Under the circumstances, however—with him being hospitalized and then as a ward of his apartment, fevered with mortality and fending off all aid—he didn't have it in him to ascertain the originating email of that Subject: whether the present missive dilated the old email about the Twin Towers, or the old email about Uncle Shoyl/Sha'ul being deceased.

Either, in their time, could've been the Bad New.

But now, healing up, that rubric seemed prophetic, despite its present usage at the top of an email that concerned itself instead with all news good and cheery, copypasted in vivid different balloon fonts: Dina wrote that Ilan, her husband, had just turned 50, which attainment the couple had celebrated with a jaunt to the Dalmatians, lately his career had been picking up steam, given the unexpectedly extensive natural gas fields recently uncovered in the Mediterranean. Meanwhile, her own career was advancing at the veterinary clinic to the point that she'd had to hire a dental aide and Yoav, their son, was about to get out of the army.

Dina got to her gravamen only at the close of the email, but made it brief, a studiedly casual request, as if typed offhand: she wrote that Yoav, she'd written *your cousin, Yoav,* who'd be discharged in the summer, was hoping to visit the States, and would it be in any way feasible—rather she'd phrased it: *if it is acceptable to you at all*—for him to come and stay in New York, *just for a time,* and then: *in return for stay with you it is so nice if you can get him also a job.*

David, still not restored to former strength, gunmetal laptop atop his stunned chest, had written back immediately—

jumping at the opportunity, jumping as if at prey: it would be his pleasure.

It was inexplicable, his agreeing—how he'd felt about Yoav coming. His avidity among the recuperative hazes, the morphine sleeps, the bland diet, no nicotine, no booze. It was a weakness of the heart. While being treated, he'd been infected with sentiment, nostalgia, a nasty nosocomial case. Out of nowhere, David had found himself yearning, but not for the immediate, for the far. Distance gave a grandeur to the emotions, expanded the dwindling self, expanded its purchase, by imbuing each desire with an ancestry, a mystery, a primitive significance, compared to which his own rehabilitation seemed a drudge: the doctors' appointments, the nurses applying electrodes, the limpness of his shaft.

It'd saddened him, how Ruth had seemed to take even his loss of sexual function in stride, or as a sign of his welcoming a deepening of their intimacy. She'd hovered, like a mother hovered.

Tammy, for her part, was unsure how to act. She was as disappointed that he'd survived as she would've been had he not.

Throughout all this, what'd bolstered him was Israel: the ideal of it, the abstraction. To have family in the country was to have the country in the family, the whole entire country. Forget the individuals, forget that Dina was a spay and neuter tyrant and Ilan a perfunctory boor, David's was a greater relationship, between his delusion and spirituality, between his ignorance and soul and so, at bottom, in that bloody chamber beneath the skin, it was a reckoning with death. If he'd stay in touch with Israel, if he'd maintain with Israel, certain responsibilities would devolve on the living after his demise. He was almost sure of it, he almost said it aloud: who among the living was going to shovel the dirt in his grave or say a kaddish? His daughter?

So that's why he'd agreed—or was it? How to judge? David could only yearn, could only crave. Until in his impotence he'd fathered a figment—his cousin arising out of his anesthesia like a son, arriving from across the seas to increase him.

He received another email from Dina, just about the time he went back to work. Still under the banner of *Bad New*, now *Re: Re:*, it consisted of a checklist of questions, detailed, persnickety questions: about what to pack, what the weather would be, about where Yoav would be housed, the nature of the work, and of the payment, if and when he'd have days off, and/or a considerable stretch of at least partially paid leave in which to travel—all of this posed to David with a manic curiosity verging on the militant, as if failing to prepare for a stint of R&R in the incredibly well-equipped, well-outfitted abundance of New York, a city in which anything forgotten from home could be bought, in which everything not for sale or even conceivable at home could be bought, was as perilous a prospect as failing to prepare for a major combat operation.

Dina was a shrewd negotiator.

For some reason, David didn't turn their talks over to Ruth, or try to interest or even inform his daughter. He felt—for some reason, he felt compelled, and responded to each bullet-pointed neurosis himself.

And it was only now that David realized that throughout all this, he'd only ever been in touch with Dina: he'd never spoken with Yoav directly.

He'd woken, as was his habit, before his alarms—he'd always prided himself on that, anticipating his alarms, cancelling them before their sounding. He was in a room. A plain singlewindowed containment of jaundiced parquet and anemic plaster. A central ceiling light domed down from the fan, light on, fan whirring.

It was the bed that threw him, its sibling furniture. All that overbearing oak, imposing, obstructing, inassimilable: Queens.

He checked Yoav's flight: still ontime.

He stopped in the hall to pluck a dustbunny and because the only trashcan was in the kitchen, slipped it in a pocket. All the lights and fans were on, ablaze. He switched them off, switched the AC unit from Medium to Low, and retrieved his jacket from a doorknob. He'd never taken off his tie.

There, at the end of the hall, what'd been his childhood bedroom had been stickered all over with unfamiliar cartoon heroes. Superheroes. Chances are the Bengali Bangladeshis had raised a boy here. He tried peeling a sticker, but part of it adhered, and he was left with just a body in a cape without a head. On the sill was a cactus, Jon and Leland must've missed it. His parents had never had plants, they wouldn't have been able to cope with even a cactus. David dipped a finger into the soil—was it supposed to be this thirsty? In the bathroom, he splashed water to his mouth, returned to the bedroom and dribbled from his lips into the pot—why do this?

He turned back and turned the AC from Low to Off.

Downstairs, in the kitchen, the chipped formica was piled with all the quarters, dimes, and nickels he'd swept up just hours ago, which he now swept up in his hands: not quite a dollar for each hour he'd slept.

Not quite three and dust.

The door: the new toplock had been installed backward, locking clockwise, but he didn't have the tools or time, so he just popped the bottom and sought the van. Though the sun had barely cleared the rooftops, there was already sweat on his hairs like dew on the blades. He revved to outbleat the lawn-mowers, downed the windows and yawned through a Yield. Forget stopping for coffee—bodegas don't do drivethru.

His businesses lived and died by time. His own lateness cost, but from customer lateness he benefited. For every ten minutes that King's Moving was late to a job, the customer got $20 off. Storage, that was like parking: one minute over the hour meant customers paid the next hour in full, one day over a month meant they paid the next week at least. This was how David made money, the same way he drove: by chiseling, like his loafered feet on the pedals were hammers and the van itself was a chisel being hammered into granite, picking out the law, picking out an epitaph. He tapped the accelerator and just the moment before his fender tapped the bumper in front, braked.

He groped for the glovebox, for his pharmorganizer: tablets and capsules, all of them regulatory, all of them moderating, reducers of clotting and coagulation, decreasers of pressure. To be healthy meant being able to swallow them dry.

He turned onto Northern Boulevard heading south. The cars seeped like spread tar and hardened into traffic. A display flashed Work Zone, then Active Work Zone, then JFK Expect Delays, and then the absurd, nearly antagonizing suggestion, Take Mass Transit. What was the city hoping to achieve? To get everyone to stop, step out of their vehicles, and slink off to a train, or the buses that beeped like geese stuck behind him?

His phone was ringing and he strapped on his headset—
"PG?"

"Brother David."

"PG, you there?"

"Here and queer, David."

"What's today like?"

"Today? High 93, low 85, humidity currently holding at
70%."

"The PIX11 forecast brought to you by Dunkin—or is it
NY1? What's her name, that weatherwoman you're in love
with?"

"The meteorologist."

"Sure—meteorology is the study of how to wear a dress
while pointing at Albany."

"They're doing lane closures on the Grand Central Parkway."

"Why don't you tell me something new for a change?"

It was the same order daily—Paul Gall calling with the
schedule, calling for judgment: Havana Fashions had changed
its mind and didn't want to just have its racks shipped, but also
wanted to have them reassembled and was wondering what
that would cost. A Platinum Level customer in Secaucus, guy
who owned stripclubs and a portapotty business, was insisting
on equipping his units with livemonitored humidors for his Co-
hibas and horizontal cellaring for his Bordeaux. Pair of guys,
junkies, had been caught living in a unit at Hunts Point, caught
and ejected, unrefunded. This woman from Fairfield, the least
pleased county in all of Connecticut, had been phoning for
days complaining that her movers broke "like a—some what
the fuck thing?"

"What the fuck, Paul?"

"Windchime—no. Windvane?"

"We broke her weathervane?"

"Tommy says we didn't."

"Tom says. That's why we have insurance."

"What about the house?"

"What about it? Thanks for taking care of the furniture."

"Classy, no?"

"Sure—you turned my parents' house into a funeralhome."

"Very tasteful."

"Anyway, my cousin. The kid. I'm picking him up just now and I want you to start putting him on shifts. Something comfortable, something easy."

"You serious, Brother D?"

"I'm serious—why? You're going to tell me that even with the summer rush the rotation's crunched? Or are you worried about him taking slots away from the regulars? Or are they worried about it—the regulars?"

"That's some of it."

"Just some?"

"The rest is my advice: you have to rest him, bench him. He'll start eventually. There's always fall. We'll need him in the fall."

"OK, coach—what's got into you? Any reason that you're talking like we're going to be short on hitters in the playoffs?"

"The kid served, no? Just finished soldiering? You're going to want to give him time to get used to being a civilian again. Like I did with Tommy after Afghanistan."

"Paul, Tom was in the Coast Guard. Afghanistan has no coast."

"Tommy was in Bagram, he was in Kandahar."

"For like a day he was, a day each at most."

"Inspecting cargo being shipped home during the drawdown. No one's more thorough than the Coast Guard."

"Tell it to the Marines. Or the Navy. Or the capos of the Gigante family."

"I'm telling you."

"What?"

"Your cousin deserves a break after what he's been through."

After David ended the call, he realized: he wasn't quite sure what that was. What exactly Yoav had been in the army. What exactly he'd done. In last summer's war. Whether he'd been a mechanic or sapper or a kevlared PR stooge, whether he was traumatized. By having been too in the action or too out of it.

The Van Wyck was a slog. He should've taken Woodhaven.

At the Linden exit, he compared the time on the dash with the time on his phone and hoped to be accommodated by the discrepancy.

Anyway, it always took at least a halfhour after landing for the passengers of an international flight to deplane and crawl through immigration, baggageclaim, customs—at least an hour, he told himself, changing lanes without a signal, for the coddled passengers to toddle off as people again, stepping decompressed from neutral transit soil to American soil—concrete to concrete, asphalt to asphalt.

At the Rockaway exit, he couldn't find his billboard—what do you expect if you don't check? And why were all the mattress jingles better than his?

His phone rang again and he turned the radio off.

"I'm disturbing you," Ruth said.

"Then why are you calling?"

"To ask how the house went, to ask how you're doing."

"Good, great."

"And to tell you I'm feeling better and your plane's just at the gate."

"Thanks. Such a help. I'm glad."

"Where are you?"

"I'm driving is where."

"You should've taken Woodhaven."

He took the turn to the airport—the road curving and bumping as underpass became overpass became underpass again—toward the Terminals.

He idled at Terminal 4 between a khaki jeep and a sunburnt sedan that was peeling. People clothed for other climates streamed out onto the asphalt and stripped.

He leaned across the gearshift and tried to guess who among them was family.

"So that's a yes?" Ruth said. "We'll get together?"

"Who now?"

"Me and you and Yoav."

"You'll be working together. Yes."

"I mean outside of work. Like for the holidays."

"He's my family. Not yours."

"Yoav's such a nice name."

"Ruth."

"I'm going to make a quilt for him."

The sedan pulled out from behind, the jeep pulled out up front. The hotel shuttles consummated their circuits.

A black suit and tie and cap chauffeur revolved out the revolvingdoors towing the luggage of his passenger, who had the same black suit and tie but lacked the cap. The passenger followed and with both hands held the placard that held his name, the placard the chauffeur must've been holding that'd told him this chauffeur was his and no one else's. And that's how it goes, David was about to say, that's the deal. Some people make a name for themselves in this world, while others stay anonymous on the other side of the tinted divider.

There was a knock at the driverside window.

"Hold on, Ruth."

The cop wasn't a cop but Security, seething in polyester livery and an oversize retroreflect vest like a jersey borrowed off the Knicks.

He said, "Why you acting like I ain't even here? Disrespecting like I ain't been telling you move on?"

David said, "But I have someone just coming out," and then he said, "Officer."

"Why you get to stay and all them can't? What's it say on the sign?"

David took off his headset, pressed for speakerphone and raised his voice: "It's my mother, Officer, she's senile. I have her on the line and she's already outside and I'm just trying to find her before she strays—say hi, Mom."

Ruth, distorted by speaker, said, "Hi, Mom."

Security said, "Keep circling."

David, and the planes above, circled. A holdingpattern of tarmacs and hangars. Chainlinked lots of cars for rent. Barbed yards beyond all mileage.

"They don't let you wait," he said.

Ruth said, "That's the city for you. It's because of the terrorism."

"You have to go around."

"Why not park?"

"Where they'd let me, that's like parking in the Hamptons."

"I think it's so kind of you to go meet him yourself. As a mother I say this. It's generous. Not to send someone—not to send me like some taxi."

"I'm always generous."

"You're always flattering yourself."

"You know what I just realized? That I wouldn't recognize my own cousin if I ran him over."

David spurned the turns for Terminals 1, 2, and 3 again, rode the inside rim of the wheeling road until the turn again for 4. Men lugged boxed flatscreens wrapped with twine taped into handles. They weren't quite Jews, too buoyant. Women on the medians were tracking with their phones, trying to disambiguate all the black Lincoln Town Cars.

"By now he must be grown."

"Don't try, Ruthie. You never met him."

"I'm just saying, don't have expectations. You're not picking up who you remember—you're not picking up a child."

"They're going to send me around for another loop."

"Make sure you feed him."

"I'm getting off—something's up here."

Port Authority cruisers sirened up ahead, dervish lights only, no wailing. Troopers wielding rifles. Humvees cordoned lanes. Traffic stopped.

The revolvingdoors revolved perpetually for no one. Then a pigeon waddled in, got trapped, flapped against the glass and, as it was turned around again, went free.

"Go, go."

Rabbis came through holding their black hats despite the breezelessness—David always automatically thought of them as rabbis though he knew that only a few of them were and that most were into realestate and ladies' hosiery and on welfare.

Then it was bootyshorts, bellytees. Acidwashed jeans and wifebeaters, sixpointed stars on chains.

"Come on, let's go."

A man, or boy, emerged plane-sweaty, rumpled in a sleeveless white vneck with way too severe of a v and a pair of collegiate gray sweatpants that hung only to the calves, canvas sneaks. He had a buzzcut. He had his mother's nose, crushed flat but spanning his face. He stopped at the gumsmacked curb, straddled his wheeled duffle and adjusted his balls.

David leaned across the opposite seat as he lowered the opposite window and yelled, "Yoav."

His cousin was darker, taller, leaner, and insensible to him. If David had been a sniper his cousin would already be dead.

"Yo Yoav, blue van, smack in front of you."

Honk.

✳

To Whom It May Concern At The Bank: My name is Maria Jesula Franklin and I am the Widow of a Husband Who died last year in a work related accident and the Single Mother of a 6 and a half year old Son Who lived with Me at 315 Broad Street, #B, Staten Island. This was the Home (apartment) My Husband owned under His own name and for which His salary paid because I am Disabled (physically) and cannot work, the Home I was going to pay off after He died with the workers comp settlement and insurance but the settlement "stalled" and the policy "lapsed"—And so this was the Home You came to seize in the middle of the night, while I was sleeping in bed with My Son. He was scared and scared Me by messing His pjs and screaming. He did not understand how You could just enter Our House like it was Yours in the night and start packing everything, start taking everything. I told Issa (My Son) to run to the Duffys (the Neighbors) and just wait for Me there. I should not have hit Him to get Him out of there, I should not have let Him get away from Me, but I was trying to gather the things. I gathered the document things and Our clothes but You did not give Me time for the Watch. You just threw me out to the hall. And I fell and You threw Me to the stairs, though I have a bubble in My head that makes it troublous to balance. The Duffys would not even let Me in their lobby, They just tossed Issa to Me and shouted, go tell it to the shelter. The shelter was a sin. I know that I did not make the mortgage and so that everything must be taken from Me, I know that I deserve this and that I have brought this on Myself, but I ask You for mercy on the Watch. The rest is Yours, I just ask for this Watch, which is not worth a chirp except to Me, with a family value. This Watch was My Husbands and His Fathers before and was kept in the back of the bottom drawer of the chest in the bedroom behind the socks. I want to give It to Issa one day, to wear on His wrist the face of His Father. Please tell Me You have It and I will come to Your branch on Bay Street to reach an arrangement. I need this Watch, because the other day My headbubbles popped and so My Son was taken away by NY Child Services. And I know, I just know, that if I get the Watch back then I will get Him back too, Issa, For every One that asketh receiveth and He that seeketh findeth and to Him that knocketh It shall be opened.

YOAV AND URI
(The Facts on the Ground)

KIVSA Brigade, Akavish Battalion, Tziraah Company, Platoon Bet, Squad Bet—the Death Alley Ewes, the Heroes of Shujaiyeh, the Martyrs of Salah al-Din Road—wasn't a special unit, just a specialish unit, not elite, but elite enough. Nothing about them made sense. Take, for instance, their name, which they'd regarded as a joke—that they were referred to as ewes, or frail female lambs—until they went into combat and the joke, like sheep's milk, went sour. They were infantry, after all, so it was difficult not to feel like sacrificial bleaters, fleecy soldiers who'd been sent off to slaughter.

Kivsa, Akavish, Tziraah.

Ewe, Spider, Wasp.

The source of this, their full unit designation, was to be found in Torah and in other venerably tedious books that were like Torah, whose legends had been introduced to them by an old—but a 40 something year old—veteran on the very first day of their training. It's strange, how your only religious training can come from the army . . . how your only religion can be the army . . .

Once there was a young shepherd boy who, because he understood everything, had been chosen by God to become the next king of Israel. This boy understood everything except why God had created the spider and why God had created the wasp. The spider weaved webs for itself but nothing for man. The wasp was not a bee and so didn't even make honey.

God counseled the boy to have patience.

And so one day this young shepherd who would be king found himself pursued by the army of the king before him. Desperate to elude capture, he ran into a cave, and just as the army approached, God sent a spider to spin its silks over the mouth of the cave, to conceal him, and so the shepherd was spared.

Later, the shepherd retaliated by raiding the enemy camp, only to be apprehended and dragged to the tent of the general. But just as he was about to be executed, God sent a wasp to sting the general, who hopped around and shrieked like a woman, and so the shepherd who would be king ran away.

To serve in a unit that bore the name of the ewes of the shepherd king, and of his spider and wasp, was supposed to be inspirational.

But the only lesson they ever took from their naming was this: they were creatures created for a single purpose, a woolly clumsy freakish creature with an excess of bristly limbs and just one measly stinger going dull through overuse.

They were useless until they were necessary.

Their unit's insignia, their official patch, was a shepherd's staff, or crook, as if to symbolize how they'd been herded together out of a number of totally unrelated and disorganized flocks. Their unofficial song was Dimona Party by DJ Skazka, featuring Avram Kaplansky. Their motto was: *Thou art the men*. Though they never used that and instead came up with their own: *Useless until necessary*.

Or, until they were discharged. Until they were redeployed, or had redeployed themselves, but as civilians.

Because this was what they did, what most of them did: they left. The moment their stints were up, they left the land they'd defended—the land they'd been conscripted by, and so it was never much of a choice, their defense.

After having served the State of Israel for 36 months, or 154 weeks, or 1,080 days, they exchanged their drabs for denims, beat their munitions into passports, and shipped beyond the sea to find their fortunes. To find themselves, or the selves they'd been, and to forget the commands that bound them.

Historically, of course, that had always been the function of exile, or diaspora. Wandering was just an emergency measure: the Jews would dwell in a country until that country expelled them, or tried to destroy them, and then they'd have to flee.

But the soldiers of Kivsa/Akavish/Tziraah/Bet/Bet weren't Jewish, or weren't exclusively Jewish—they were also, primarily, Israeli, which meant they just served their compulsory tours in their nation's armed forces until they were at liberty to book tickets abroad. All the fit, tanned, 21-year-old vets who could afford it, or whose families could afford it, would mark the conclusion of their military service by going on a holiday that ever since First Lebanon—their parents' last war—had come to feel as compulsory as that service itself, as if vacationing were merely war's covert continuation, an undercover mission camouflaged in sportsgear.

And though backpacking between the better hostels of East Asia will never be as dangerous as bulldozing hovels in the West Bank, there was still the chance of not coming back, or not coming back alive.

———

They were in Kathmandu and drunk on rice, stumbling through the earthquake rubble.

They were in Patan, where they bought this stinky local leaf that didn't fuck them up, the way they'd been promised it would fuck them up, and when they brought what was left of it back to the old man noncombatant who'd sold it to them, he put up his hands and showed with a smack of his toothless mouth: don't smoke, chew.

They were in Pokhara, where they bumped into a bivouac of guys from Border Patrol, who despite being Border Patrol knew their way around, and took them to visit whores, who despite being stumpy native whores knew how to say all the nasty shit that can't be said in Hebrew, and how to do all the nasty shit that can't be done by Jews, and two of the guys—not their guys, the other guys—told the girls that they were virgins, but the truth was that four of them were virgins, and for an extra 5,000 rupees, roughly 180 shekels, condoms weren't required.

The girls had a misguided trust in the circumcised.

They were up in the Himalayas and marching, they were hiking, and the flatness steepened, and the steepness flattened, and they settled into a count. Everything had been planned like it used to be, except that now they'd planned it for themselves: they'd mapped everything out, set their own mealtimes and resttimes, the kilometers to cover, decided the alternate routes, deferring to one another by specialty and rank, but then the elevation and landscape changed so that no specialties applied and the ranks fell away like a boulder. The mountains seemed no closer. The mountains seemed cut out of the sky. They went ahead in formation, singlefile in the narrows, becoming part-nered again as the ways went wide, vigilant for the slightest disturbance, a hostile blur or rustle. Thorong La would be theirs by Shabbat, the Annapurna massif would be in their hands, and they'd plant their flag at the peak of the pass, claim-ing everything unto the Tibetan plateau in the name of Pvt Shlomo "Shlo" Regev, who'd been hit in the face by a mortar near the Erez border crossing—in Gaza.

After their discharge some of Kivsa/Akavish/Tziraah/Bet/Bet stuck together, some struck out on their own:

Avi went to Mexico, to export electronics. Binyamin went to Canada, to import electronics. Yaniv was trekking the Amazon. Chaim was living with a paddleboard in Thailand, or with a sailboard in Cambodia, or dwelling homeless and shoeless like a monk in Vietnam, weaving baskets out of bamboo just for the therapy—he was like a loose reed himself, blown along the coast between Hanoi and Ho Chi Minh.

And Micki's conquering Paris, Amir's laying siege to Berlin. Moti and Dani are storming Warsaw, having left Cracow in smoldering ruins.

Eli . . .

was bumming around India, the beaches. Full moon parties, new moon parties. Each phase got its own rave in Goa. Not that Eli was noticing the phases. MDMA was keeping the sun in his eyes and turning his ears into conches. At a club in Karwar, an

83

Irish guy had called him a dirty Arab, and after Eli had said he was a dirty Israeli, the guy called him a kike, and Eli took a swing at the guy, and then the rest of the guy's Irish stag group materialized and Eli had to leave, to leave the state. He went to Kerala, to Kochi, and followed the tides. He still stayed in excellent shape. And stayed very active online, sharing updates on wave conditions, and posting about how to keep fit on the go, @ imshi-eli94.jutube.co.il.

Sami . . .

who'd made aliyah at two years old from Soviet Russia, traveled back to the new Russia, only to realize his parents hadn't lied: Moscow was disgusting, St. Petersburg was snobbish, and the language he'd spoken at home in Petah Tikva wouldn't be enough to get by—it was a two year old's. Waitresses, shopclerks, anyone left who recalled his parents, all laughed at him, resented him—they refused to pity the lucky yid, who'd escaped. He'd been the squad's best marksman, and its only soldier to wear a yarmulke, knitted black and the size of a bulletwound from a Galatz SR-99. Soon he was going around bareheaded, sitting at cafés, filling out applications and remediating for the entrance exams to the Technion (no chance), University of Haifa (no chance), Afeka College of Engineering (maybe), Holon Institute of Technology (maybe), smoking cigarettes, drinking cognacs, ordering ham pirozhki and getting fat, and developing this suspicion that he was balding too, and with each turned page of his trigonometry textbook he was rubbing his skull, wondering what if anything was missing.

Natan . . .

who'd been the squad's commander, a Sergeant FC, and a recipient of the Medal of Distinguished Service, had resettled

himself in London. He'd enrolled in some degree program offered by some online university that, once he'd finished it,
would entitle him to a promotion, though not to a promotion
with raise, from the job he'd been working since arriving at
Heathrow—from security guard to security supervisor, for El
Al. The new title would register impressively on a resume, especially on a bilingual resume printed out on thick heavy off-
white paper, though all it'll mean is that instead of screening
the luggage he'll be screening the guards who screen the luggage. Eventually, he'll be moved up to a desk. Next, he might
even be transferred to an office of his own, and maybe not even
at Heathrow, maybe at El Al HQ in London proper, in Blooms-
bury. For a while, though, he'll still be four credits shy, and
then, for a while, two credits. He'll be nervous, because he
won't be able to afford the credits, but then his employer will
pay for the class. He'll start screwing a classmate, a sturdy
pretty Brit with brown hair, round face, big freckled tits, and a
big pale ass, and he'll send the rest of the squad photos of her,
and videos of them together, some taken with her consent,
some definitely taken without, and others that it'll be hard to
judge just which.

———

And then there was him: Yoav Matzav. Present and accounted
for.

It'd been about four months since the army had dismissed
him and whichever of the others had survived, and about two
since he'd forsaken the State of Israel for the States. Or, according to the cablebox's coordinates, which he'd crossrefer-
ence with the TV's, he'd already been out of Israel for one

month, two weeks, three days, four hours, say—he was never any good at calculating the seven hour time difference.

He'd spent that time on the couch, which was big, with big smelly flowers on it, wilted in the frame, lumpy in the cushions, ugly.

Still, Yoav slept there, not up in the bed. Or, he'd been trying to sleep.

The first moving he did—the first night of his stay, before he was put to work, and so this was just a simulation or practice moving—was to move this couch to the center of the room and remove its plastic slipcover, which he used as a blanket and napkin. To have established so central a redoubt—no longer up against any walls, no longer flush with any other furniture—was to be exposed but also exposing.

He understood and accepted the risks: you had to make yourself vulnerable to make out your perimeters, to protect your flanks, 360° all around.

It was the only place he felt at home, in all the house around him.

It's where he did everything, where he woke.

He'd go to the bathroom, and come back to the couch. He'd go to the kitchen for a beer, and come back to the couch. He'd go to the kitchen again for a light from the stove, and come back to the couch and smoke. Even if he got up from the couch to go to the bathroom and was finished with the beer now sloshing with ash and had to bring it back to the kitchen to trash it out, he wouldn't take it, he'd just leave it, only so that he had to come back to the couch after the bathroom and relax, just relax, before he got up again and went to the kitchen and laid the ashy can of Bud atop the trash, which he never bothered to empty, he never even put in a bag.

He sat with his computer and tried reading the news in English, but always returned to the Hebrew sites, and sat on the phone with his mother, who'd just woken up too, trying to tell her how to chat him—"Add me to Contacts, achla," "Click my name to add me to Contacts, sababa"—telling her to get his father to show her.

"I just want to hear you and see you, the both at once," she kept saying, "is that from America too much to ask?"

He was using a neighbor's signal, which was unreliable—all of his neighbors' signals were either unreliable or protected by password, and many times, especially in the mornings, but Israel's mornings, his mother's voice would crackle and her image, midgrimace, would freeze.

He'd be cut off like just another unplugged appliance in this house of so many appliances, so much drawerandcabinetstuff, all crammed.

In the kitchen there were enough placesettings for a family, as if Cousin David were telling him through crockery what his parents—what his mother, not his father—had always told him verbally, that one day he'd have to start a family of his own. There were three coffeemakers, two teakettles, and an unlidded pot that didn't immediately advertise its use. He was confused by it, by the bouquet of skewers sticking out of it, though it was only a pot for fondue. He thought the letters along its scoured metal side might be forming a word, he thought the word was just the name of the manufacturer of . . . whatever it was, but it was just the monogram of its former owner . . .

Yoav sat tossing the skewers like pygmy spears into this un-
identifiable pot that reminded him of the helmet of a van-
quished knight and some would land inside with a coining clank
and some would miss and go skidding and after he'd tossed
them all he'd get up and retrieve them.

And then come back to the couch.

The couch was where he ate his cutlets not from the closer
Open For 24 Hours Deli, but from the farther Open For 12
Hours Deli, where he bought or tried to buy his Buds and
Marlboros too, because the farther Open For 12 Hours Deli
was Mexican, and the closer Open For 24 Hours Deli was Syr-
ian, and on his initial visit its cashier had by default addressed
him in Arabic, to which he'd responded, likewise by default, in
his rudimentary service Arabic, and in the interrogation that
ensued had represented himself as Ismail the itinerant carpen-
ter from Al-Quds—he'd usurped the identity of one of his
squad's former informers, just to hear himself do it, to see if he
could do it, if he could get away with it, or merely to justify his
patronage.

Each time he'd leave the house, it was only to complete a
single errand, which was all he could manage—one roll toiletpaper, one bar soap, that's all he could take—before he had to
return to his cushioning.

Sunday Trashday Tuesday Wednesday Trashday Friday Sat-
urday, but on the occasions that Cousin David would pick him
up, Yoav had to clean, at least the groundfloor, because that's as
far as his cousin would venture, just to pick up the mail, which
was bills, and turn down, or off, the AC. One day, Cousin David
took him to the Statue of Liberty and Ellis Island and the World
Trade Center Memorial, all in one day, and in the evening

wanted to take him to a sushi and hibachi restaurant, but wanted him to change his clothes and told him to be quick about it and waited outside in the van and even though his cousin was waiting Yoav sat, just for a moment, before going upstairs and getting dressed, and then he sat again quickly after.

He'd sit, remote in hand, triggerfingering, until telling night from day from screen was getting as difficult as pointing out Zion on a spinning globe.

Cousin David would parade him around like a hero, for a weekend straight of cooing Jews, then drop him.

Though Yoav wasn't quite able yet to discriminate between weekends and weekdays, American goyim and American Jews—Israel took off Fridays and Saturdays, the States took off Saturdays, Sundays, and apparently the rest of the summer.

It was still summer. Same smog, stagnancy, clinging.

David was driving him in the van over a bridge and said, "Sorry again for not getting the porch repaired."

"OK," Yoav said. He understood, at least, that this was an apology.

"No pressure, but maybe while we're waiting to put you on shifts, you can try repairing it yourself?"

"Maybe."

"We have the lumber in Jersey, the sealant. Or forget it—I'll get the guys out."

"Say to the guys I work with them. To move."

But David said, as God said to the shepherd king, "Be patient."

Life had become as confusing to Yoav as the tenses and persons of the auxiliary verb *to be*, which is to say he was dismayed to find that his English—despite years of mandatory instruction in school, months of private lessons with a Bible studies PhD from Exeter visiting Israel to research Christ, repeated encounters with every episode of every season of *Sex and the City* (subtitled), sporadic encounters with *Fast & Furious 1–6* (undubbed), and an aborted reading of the collected works of Sherlock Holmes (abridged)—sucked:

"I patient."

"What?"

His Exeter/Devonshire/American media mongrel accent, like that of an effeminate Berber pirate, wasn't helping matters: Oi PAY-shun.

"When I was younger," David said, "I certainly wasn't. I couldn't stop myself—I couldn't get enough."

He sheared the van into a tunnel. Yoav shut his eyes.

"There a girl on your mind? Or you just tired, Yo?"

Yoav was tunneling into himself, begging in breaths to be back aboveground and in the clement light.

"Buck up. A boy like you, you'll meet someone here—she'll meet you."

As they rode into the sun again, Yoav exhaled and said, "This all also Manhattan?"

David took a hand off the wheel and thumbed. "That was Manhattan, behind us. That nightmare we just drove through."

Yoav turned around toward the city.

"Work, women and work," David said. "I'll be honest, at a certain age it catches up with you and you want something else. You want that profound connection. But you can't get it, not with a bank letter, not even with cash. Retail or wholesale, a profound connection's just not on the market. Because the

truth is, you have it already, it's there for you, it's yours, whenever you're willing to accept it—if you have a family, you've had
it all along."

"Yes."

"We're family, Yo."

"I thinking yes."

"Keep thinking," David said. "Next time we'll get Tammy
out."

Yoav yawned. They thudded through the suburbs.

"All my life I worked at this one thing harder than I worked
at anything else. You know what that was, Yo? It was being a
Jew. It was proving I was. People who thought I was greedy—
I took from. People who thought I was pushy—I pushed. But
anyone under the impression I was gentle and wise, I came to
them in the spirit of lovingkindness. You understand?"

"Who say to you this?"

"It's not important. In this business, everyone talks. My point
is, unlike me, Yo, you're a real Jew. This is who you are natu-
rally, grown up from the land. And now that you've paid your
dues to that land, now that you've suffered for the state, you're
out, you're here, and you have to understand the significance.
Here in America, a real Jew like you is going to have to find his
own thing to prove."

And off they went to another cookout. Yoav liked corn on the
cob, he was ambivalent about pie.

*

The only reason Yoav was in the States, the truest deepest only reason he was able to lounge, loathe, and develop opinions about why goyim or just Jews in the States made such disproportionate use of sunblock, was because the summer before, almost one year to the day before he landed in New York, in the midst of what foreign press were calling the Gaza War, or the Second Gaza War, or the Third Gaza War, which Israel was once again insisting was only a conflict—*Operation Firm Cliff* or *Resolute Cliff* was the literal Hebrew, which made the violence seem Biblically wrathful, *Operation Protective Edge* was the official English obligingly supplied by the IDF, which made the violence seem warranted because merely prophylactic—his friend, Uri, had saved his life.

His friend and squadmate, Corporal Uri Dugri—who, like a score of their other squadmates, both alive and dead, now remained behind in Israel:

Kosta was tending to his cancerous parents in Netanya,

Gad was preparing to matriculate at Hebrew University (the Faculty of Humanities),

Reuven was preparing to reenlist in the army as a cadet in the Officers' Training Course (Bahad 1),

Menachem was settling into work at his family's rubber processing concern and trying to get his girlfriend to be his wife or just pregnant in Herzliya,

Eitan and Oded were in Tel Aviv trying to scrape together the cash to open up a studio devoted to their new form of martial arts, which had 42 defensive stances, 168 offensive stances, but as of yet no coherent philosophy.

Uri, meanwhile, was sitting around in his childhood bedroom in Nika just jerking it.

Rather, he was devoting all of his considerable energies to not jerking it, to keeping his hands off his cock—because at any moment one or two or three of his older sisters might come crashing through the door in storms of wet hair and nails—to check on him, to call him for meals, to ask him about their hair, nails, outfits, and boys as pretexts for checking on him, to nag him about his own romantic prospects now that everything with Batya Neder was in absolute collapse—"That girl was like a wall," they liked to say, "with no curves and the chin of a Firm or Resolute Cliff"—giving him advice but no privacy, never any peace . . .

Such were . . . ha'uvdot b'shetach, "the facts on the ground": that Uri was still grounded in Israel, that he was living again with his family and unable to relocate out of a lack of imagination or shekels or both, that he was in the process of cutting himself off from his only friends, his squadmates, out of the shame of being the only one of them to have left the army with no education arranged, no employment set up, and headaches that the miracle rabbi his mother would send him to—that even the Psycholog his sisters would send him to, unbeknownst to their mother, who wouldn't have approved—would dismiss as every bit as psychosomatic as his dreams. Which wouldn't stop the dreams, or make them taper, or deny their legitimacy, their truth.

Even Rotem, who'd lost his legs and was in a wheelchair, would wheel himself to their monthly squad reunions . . . Even Dror would show, despite his oxygen tank, for which he'd quit smoking, for which he'd quit drinking . . .

Uri was the only one missing, the only one who'd skip. He was too busy not returning their emails. Having anger issues, putting fists through walls. Mortaring closet doors, bareknuckled. His parents had been whispering together so he wouldn't understand. Arabic, but a sophisticated dated Arabic, was becoming—as it'd been under the reign of his Moroccan grandparents—the higher language of the house.

His mother had gotten Uncle Peretz, a senior warder in the Israel Prison Service, to get him an interview for the guard program, but he'd missed the deadline to register, and then he'd missed the extended deadline, and since then, his mother's crying. His father had brought him along on a roofing job, but by week's end his dizziness was such that he'd had to step down the ladder and leave, and since then, his father's howling.

Crying and howling were Arabics too, which were still happier than the chastening he got from Batya Neder.

Uri had grown up with Batya and loved her and made the motions of love to her in a field. But because the army requires all men to serve for three years and women for two, she'd already been out for one, and in just that one had managed to leave pitiful Nika for Tel Aviv, enroll on scholarship in a computer academy, get recruited by a man to join his firm, which developed or just adapted apps, and—don't think about it—to share the man's apartment, his duplex.

The Batya Uri had known had been a pretty athletic Teimaniyah (Yemenite), not a sedentary coder. She must've picked up that computing interest in the army (in Intelligence), and yet she'd never mentioned it in all the txts she'd sent, the fewer and fewer txts, or on any of the brief occasions their leaves coincided. He'd also never known her to hang up on him. Their last conversation he'd tried to stay on nonerotic terms, which she'd initiated. She'd been filling him in on her life, but that single word, or the fact that he hadn't recognized that word and had asked her to repeat it, and then had asked her to explain it, and she'd laughed, had set him off into a rage. It wasn't even Hebrew, or it hadn't been until Batya and others like her had made it Hebrew: duplex.

"What do you mean—others like me?" she'd said.

Others like people who go to coed computer academies. Or people who cohabitate with their instructors and speak fancy languages and make fancy salaries and have copious oral sex at artistic parties in Tel Aviv.

"You'd better get out of Nika," she'd said.

Nika was a dusty moshav halfway between Kiryat Gat and Beersheva and so halfway between nowhere and not quite somewhere. The place barely existed and yet was impossible to leave. This was because it was laid out in a concentric circling, like a target's roundel or the crosshaired reticle of a telescopic sight, with roads that compassed around and around and around and never intersected. To get to the bullseye, which was just a runty stucco administrative office that also held pesticides, you had to walk through people's orchards, through people's gardens. Past the outer rim road were the communal fields: the fields that were in every way identical because all-encompassing, or in every way identical because always changing, with crops and clearings appearing and disappearing seasonally, so that to get Batya alone Uri had always had to do some reconnaissance, some fieldwork, and remember the location of a certain cleared space, and hope that it would remain clear for however long it would take him to check the school, or the silos, or the aquifers, for her—for however long it would take him to coax her. He recalled that spring patch where he'd laid Batya down for the first and she'd run away, leaving him to grind into the soil and spew himself, panting. He recalled that autumn patch to which he'd dragged her, a harvest and two acne regimens later, and to which he'd dragged along a blanket and spread it out and spread her out atop it. The blanket was from his bed—he'd rolled her in it, rolled her wrapped in her clothes and then just in her hair. She had tiny hairs on her ass like browned grass. Tiny brown anthill tits but gangling nipples like carob pods. An ant had crawled up from an ear and across a closed eyelid and she'd felt the crawl and wouldn't open up. That blanket they'd used, the same child's blanket that still covered his bed, had remained blue even when the sky itself hadn't and the only indications of all the sweat and time that'd elapsed since then was that the white of its cloud pattern was pilling and her bloodspot had yellowed.

Now he'd just sit with legs wedged under the bed, window shut, curtains drawn, lights off, naked so as to deter any entering sorority, naked except for his stubble (buzzcut growing out,

unibrow grown out), aviator sunglasses tangling with his
unibrow—and there in that stifling darkness he'd do situps
(crunches, bicycle and butterfly and regular). He'd lie, with his
feet wedged under the dresser, his feet lifting the dresser to
just before the point at which it'd tip and fall atop and crush
him. Candidates for guard in the Israel Prison Service had to
be able to complete at least 50 regular crunches in a minute or
less. Candidates for guard in the Israel Military Prison Service
had to complete 70. Uri was averaging 100, and 30 pullups
(hands in), 30 chinups (hands out), 65 each of pushups and
crossedleg pushups and knuckle pushups. He lifted the weights
he'd made for himself on that construction site, the weights
being his only accomplishment on that construction site besides quitting—on his first day taking two withered Alliance
tires from their roadside desertion and a metal showercurtain
rod from the trashbin of the neighboring property and insert-
ing the rod through the holes in the tires and mixing the cement and pouring the cement into the holes and waiting for it
all to harden like his heart, and so it did, by close of day, and he
went home, his father had driven him home, with a perfectly
decent barbell clunking around in the trunk, which he now
lifted and pressed and curled and rowed in many reps of many
sets, until his compact apeface was drenched to the neckbeard
and he'd banished from his brain that kid from Gaza City from
whom he'd annexed the idea: that kid who'd lost his lower jaw
who'd kept his barbells like this in the livestock pit that'd passed
for his backyard—that'd passed for his backyard even before
the war.

Uri would workout until his sisters burst in or he was de-
feated by sleep. He dreamt of cities and burnwards, of his mid-

dle sister Orly sneaking into his room and spraying this rancid green aerosol in his eyes to give him nightvision and in his ears to give him nighthearing and all over his body to armor it and give him nighttouch. The way he exercised, it was like he was planning something. He squatted like he dreamt, like a man pursued.

What he was proudest of was that his arm muscles and leg muscles were equally developed and that, when it came to his arms, his biceps and triceps were equally impressive. He hadn't made that common amateur's mistake of neglecting one set of fibers in favor of another and, when adrift in refractory moments, had the tendency to keep a hand on one or the other, left arm or right, biceps or tri, gripping it, pumping it like a flotation device, packing it like a parachute, kneading it like bread.

This was the same process, it turned out, required to stuff and button all his newish bulk into his shirts and pants from before the army. To cram himself into shoes, the type of shoes where you have to wear socks—you have to polish.

Uri had been granted an audience with the Baba Batra, that most famous of diminutive rabbis, or that most diminutive of famous rabbis, depending on whom you asked. It was a privilege you had to dress up for, you had to make a donation. Uri was dreading it, but his mother gave him no choice: she swore by this wonderworking sage who'd brought babies to barren friends, quelled a cousin's Armenian fever, and eradicated Tay-Sachs from the family genes. Uri's sisters wished him luck, but tartly, and darted off to class, which meant something different to each of them: cosmetology class, merchandising class, the mall.

Uri's father—a tolerant skeptic who always drove Uri's mother to work, dropping her off first even if his current construction site was closer to home than her tailoring job at a bridal emporium—dropped Uri off at a modernist, but ancient modernist, faith complex in Netivot of six stone tents resembling a vivisected star.

Bustling men in white—asylum orderly but also piously white—passed his cash, his name, and his person down halls, left him sitting, to wait.

There was no one ahead of him, there was no one behind, but still: there was waiting. A condition so chronic, so messianically anticipant, that its trappings didn't matter. Sometimes you waited at home in your room so demobilized into quiet that you could just about feel the maskingtape losing its stick and your mortifying teenaged posters of American moviestars who were 50% Jewish and Argentinian-German models who were 100% hot, Uri Malmilian (the football striker), Uri Geller (the mentalist), and Ha'Tzanchanim (the Paratroopers), peeling slowly from the walls, and sometimes you waited away from home in a room cluttered up with pews and vociferous copies of *Yom Le'Yom, Maariv,* and *National Geographic,* which mocked with all the exotic destinations in which your friends were becoming themselves, or themselves as other people, as bicycle messengers, yoga instructors, contractors in Sudan, pure—and sometimes you waited in no rooms at all, just out in the cold sun, blanking.

He'd waited in yards, in tents, in trailers converted to offices: in line. At the Lishkat Ha'Giyus, the Recruitment Bureau, he'd stood for his physical, a stethoscope cupping his back just below its sole tuft of hair. His face was photographed (no smiling), his teeth were photographed (in case his face got mangled). His fingerprints were taken and then two young Persian women took his damp hands into theirs and one told him to turn to her and he did and the other woman stabbed him and so he turned around to her and the woman who'd spoken stabbed him too, inoculating him against tetanus, meningitis, hepatitis, flu, and trust.

He sat waiting for his haircut, as curls tumbled like desert weeds across the floor and earrings were removed from the people around him, and because the guys doing the shaving and earring removal were fans of a rival team, Hapoel Jerusalem, they joked about eliminating this other guy's Beitar Jerusalem tattoo by skinning him with their razors.

He filled in the bubbles of the psychometric exams, grasping for analogies, grasping at the math. Among mankind's greatest faults is his a) kindness, b) generosity, c) fortitude, d) contentment, e) vanity. That was debatable. But the Pythagorean theorem was not, and if the civilian Uri was one side and the soldier Uri was the other, the true him was the hypotenuse, slanted opposite, the squared sum of both.

He waited for his ride to the Bakum, the Induction Base, and waited out the ride, counting the kilometers on his way to playing other games with puzzles, blocks, and balls, which he would've enjoyed except that they kept him away from the sweltry hut he shared with a gang of rowdy arsim—swaggering Mizrahim descended from families like his that'd fled Casablanca, or been tossed out of Algiers, Tunis, Benghazi, and Baghdad and so who hated the Arabs, but in that special covetous way only a brother hates a brother. They fought over who was the most Arab, meaning the most cruel, but also the coolest, the best, and never kept their shirts on, or their pants on, stroked semen into one another's boots, and reveled in the license of their youth and the exacting lunacy of their circumstances by beating one another to the ground.

One noon, Uri was called away from that roughhousing and brought to a climatized shed for an interview. Officers asked him what placements he wanted, which is to say they were asking who he wanted to be, and so he answered them: either Duvdevan or Sayeret Matkal, the dark stuff, the hushed stuff, counterterrorism ops, or, above all, he wanted to be a Tzanchan, he wanted to jump out of a plane—only to be told that his answers were useless, rather that if they were useful in any way it was only insofar as they provided ancillary snippets of psychological data for his profile.

That would be the last blast of full information he'd get in the army—the rest would be need to know, guesswork, divining: why he'd been placed in the unit he'd been placed in, why the others who'd gotten the same placement had gotten it, and what if anything that might say about him. Because the army never made mistakes. It never failed or lapsed. Each soldier got the assignment he deserved, rather each assignment got the soldier, and if your M16, M4, Galil, or Tavor overheated or jammed, even that was merited too, the malfunctions were intended: to prevent friendly fire or a wrongful slaughter. If your chute didn't open, or your engine stalled, or your wings fell off, it was better that way: there were reasons. Nothing ever happened out of whim or caprice. Everything was logical, logistical, systematic, each mission backed by a sacrosanct wisdom to which the average grunting soldier would never be privy. The army was a family, the officers were parents, the soldiers their kids: they received instructions, not explanations, the tactics, not the strategies, and the only way to ever survive this regime was to stop seeking its meanings and just submit, subordinate— surrender.

Imagine this vast staff of shadowy relations that keeps claiming to know what's best for you, or to know what you'd be best at, through the practice of an official magic, an authoritative mysticism involving myriad complex batteries of mental and physical tests, interviews, background checks, and just standard fulltime surveillance, whose sole objective was to uncover from within the body, mind, and soul of an 18 year old virgin his deepest essential competencies, native ingenuities, and capacities for development—the trail or path for which he'd always been intended. If a soldier was happy with the match that was made for him, then all the magic was true, the mysticism was science, and the organization responsible was close to divine, but if a soldier was unhappy, then the entire system was bankrupt, debunked, and he'd feel like he was losing his religion. This was the first lesson of the army, then, or the first that Uri retained, in the lull before his assignment: that were his wishes ever to be taken into account, the whole edifice would crumble. It was only by ignoring preferences that the theology endured.

Let the weak be disappointed—Uri was strong and would grow into any situation, like that invasive species of cactus, the pricklypear, which had been imported from South America to flourish in the desert at the fringes of the base: the sabra, it was called.

Let his fake gangster hutmates flex their pecs that were like the pads of the sabra and grumble about not becoming para-

troopers or pilots—let them weep over not being, over officially not being, what they'd been convinced they were at core:
paratrooper or pilot material. That was an ugly delusion, though
not uncommon among such overconfident prickly youths who
came out of the rougher poorer neighborhoods afflicted with
bad eyesight, bad hearing, and mild scoliosis. Who, in a country
you can't drive out of, doesn't want to fly? Or at least want to
take a submarine and surface near Ibiza?

A week later, though it'd felt like a month, Uri had his quali-
fication: his suspicions about himself, his incipient uniqueness,
had been confirmed, and he'd been granted a gibush—a next
level tryout for the special forces, the eliter commandos.

He was bussed to another facility, spent a sleepless indeter-
minacy he regarded as a week getting shrieked at and walloped,
bushwhacking up hills, up scrabbly mountains, wading through
bramble and thorn with a rockfilled pack. Each day, a handful
of guys would drop out. Or be drummed out. Because of broken hands or feet, broken minds.

Uri's story was this: once, after they'd rappelled themselves
from a particularly strenuous freeclimb ascension, everyone
was groveling sloppy with their uniforms untucked, and the
drill instructor decided to make an example, he decided to
make Uri an example, and so gathered a fistful of his shirttails
and jammed the fabric below his belt into his pants, until the
faggot was gripping Uri's dick, he was twisting. Uri keeled. And
then got up. And punched the faggot and kept punching, at all
his fellow candidates, at every drill instructor at the facility,
every officer in the country—the Defense Minister, the Prime
Minister, the President, every living member of the Knesset: it
took all of them to take him down.

That, at least, was the indignant yet aggrandizing tale he told the squad to which he was remanded the following month: Kivsa/Akavish/Tziraah/Bet/Bet.

He'd shown up, toward the conclusion of its basic training, horridly scraped at neck and knees. His cheeks were still puffy and tender. The clinic had been an incarceration, so sterile and tranquilized that even the infantry was preferable. He was in the infantry now.

He was in Kivsa/Akavish/Tziraah/Bet/Bet, specifically, because it was short a member: this Shimshon the others had barely known—because they hadn't been together long enough to know him, as anything other than a chunky South African— had been climbing a ladder during an obstacle, fallen off, and shattered his pelvis. The ladder had been positioned by his training partner and squad opinion was still split as to whether it was all the partner's fault.

Even if it wasn't his fault, Yoav, the partner who now became partners with Uri, was the worst soldier in the squad. Uri, to compensate, became the best soldier, meaning he never directly questioned whether their pairing was a punishment or compliment.

If during their initial krav maga scrimmages he fought as normal and choked Yoav out fast, immediately fast, during subsequent matches he let up and let Yoav thrash all his glib lanky body for each round's full duration.

Uri had realized that by hurting his opponent, he'd only hurt himself—they still had years to go together and there was no way to rush the time.

But then there was no impatience like that of a graduating recruit standing at attention to be sworn in at the Kotel, while the Chief Rabbi, this squinting screeching Ashkenaz, went on amplifying his remarks with misquotations of the vicious minor prophets.

After the swearing, saluting, and flag worship, they were finally soldiers, and they flung their berets into the air and then scrambled to scoop them up and put them back on: you can't stand at the Kotel without keeping your head covered.

The field days followed in procession: indomitably hot stretches of sentry duty spent just clenching bowel and bladder and greasing your gun, the perspiration coursing, as you stooped, drooped, and melted—the country was melting. The borders shrunk, expanded, kept being moved, until you found yourself trapped between where yesterday's had been and tomorrow's would be—until you, yourself, had become the border, dug into sand along roads rived by rebar and garbled with barbedwire. This was a checkpoint, between Israel and a land Palestinians called Palestine and Israelis called Judea and Samaria, because Jews can't agree on anything, they can't even agree with themselves and so both names were used. Formerly called the West Bank, though it's located just east of the country, about 40 billion of the old Canaanite cubits in psychological distance but also only 40 kilometers as the rockets fly, from where the rockets were flying from Gaza. But here you saw none, here you heard none. You just were. Put here, like you'd been put here on earth, to reinforce the patrols. Given all the recent unrest and skirmishing.

The border felt, from the outset, like a demotion. A disparagement. A squandering. The lines were endless. The days were endless lines. A checkpoint just marks the middle, the sandbagged roadblocked middle, of endless vallar lines. Palestinian workers going to, coming from, the factories in the Israeli industrial zones. Palestinian shepherds coming and going, to graze and water their flocks. Maids heading from Bethlehem to clean at the factories when what they should've been cleaning weren't the factories but Bethlehem. A woman who wasn't a maid trying to cross using the ID of her sister who was a maid but had a tumor that was preventing her from working and the family couldn't afford to lose the job. From dawn to dusk checking IDs. Checking permits. Car papers. Fucking sheep papers, as the sheep just shat and pissed. Some days the orders were to let only a certain number through, or a certain designation through, or not to let any through, at certain times. Some days you just invented the orders. You had to act as if your presence here was permanent and your authority just another element of the surrounding inarable wastes. If you convinced yourself, then you convinced the people crossing, and if you convinced the people crossing, then you convinced the wastes. That you were as rooted as the olive trees. As elemental as the clays.

There were Palestinian police, on the Palestinian side. And Israeli police, on the Israeli side. Your role, as army, was to police the police. To relay the irreconcilability of all their orders. To scan the plates. Get the driver and all passengers out of the car, their arms and legs spread and hijabs off. Put the mirror under the car like you're checking it for breath. Check the trunk and under the hood, the interior. Check the fluids. You had to be, at once, a soldier, a greasemonkey, and the angel of death. You had to be a brother and a son, even after you were relieved and took your turn in the booth using a contraband cellphone to call your parents, who were slumped in a bunker underground, eating Bissli, drinking Coke, and squabbling—

toggling the TV between Sport 5 carrying Maccabi Tel Aviv vs. FC Basel and Channel 1 with its screenblue sky and the smoke of Qassam rockets crazing through like static.

Occasionally there'd be some Hasidic rabbinic or rabbiesque figure bearing down the settlement road in his dovegray Mercedes Benz 190 between the industrial zone and the settlement on the ridge above the shepherd village and his windows would be downed and with a shake of his payos he'd be screaming at you for making him late and the funny thing would be that every once in a while the guy, because he was a Jewish transplant from America, would be doing all that screaming in English, which Uri wouldn't understand, or would only half understand, and he'd speak to the guy in Hebrew, which the guy wouldn't understand, or would only half understand, and the guy would just keep shouting something in English so that Uri would have to get Yoav to moderate the languages, if only to keep from just slapping the guy, which was never advisable, not because the guy was a Jew, or an American, or possibly an Israeli citizen, or a Hasid who resembled a rabbi, or possibly even a bonafide rabbi ordained, but because he was a settler, and as a soldier Uri was basically his employee—basically his bodyguard.

Occasionally there'd be a protest to break up, to break up the monotony: Palestinian and even Israeli, but then occasionally there'd be a few Israelis out at the Palestinian protests and everything would get confusing.

Then maybe there'd be some kid at some protest who'd maybe hurled a rock and you'd try not to shoot him, even though your gun only had rubber bullets, even though you'd been so bored you'd spent all your day crushing the rubber bullets up into small sharp pebbles so that while the rules would be respected and no laws would be broken, the skin would be, the skin would be pierced.

In general, you tried not to hit kids and women—anyone who made a fuss if they were hit: journalists.

Every once in a while there'd be a midnight run through a village just to light it up. Searching for someone. Or for no one. Finding someone else. Or no one. Going into a house, to surprise the house behind it, to surprise the neighbors nextdoor. Taking the doors off and going room to room. Herding a family into the kitchen and then heading upstairs to ransack the closets and unscrew all the beds nut by bolt. Slashing up the divan in the den and then sitting down on the framed remains to cruise the news on Al Jazeera. Or playing PlayStation. Or Wii. Awaiting further instruction, awaiting Intelligence. Babysitting a son or brother bound to the divan with plasticuffs draining him white and a drenched towel over his face keeping him cool, until the interrogators came. On your way out, confiscating bangles for your sisters, candlesticks and goblets, checkered boards for every game involving kings. A woman keening in the kitchen to the pitch of boiling water, you shut her up with the butt of your gun. You butted a jug and it sharded apart into archaeology even before it hit the floor.

The time after action was different from the time before— you couldn't wait to be sent into Gaza, but then once you got out, you could wait again forever.

The wait to be discharged—should you be feeling so impatient? The wait to get on with the rest of your spared life—why be in such a hurry to get hustled and now have to pay for your own lodging, meals, and clothes?

But still the army dragged on. With debriefings, memorial services. Notching the days with a pocketknife on the shankbone of a lamb, which you were trying to carve into a dagger. Dribbling your shadow like a football across the halfline, leaving your dead in the dust running wretched behind you, running out the clock, fouling toward the goal.

The news in Israel was about Israel being condemned by the news of other countries, the countries for which your squadmates were about to depart. And so the main topic of squad conversation, besides pussy, and Ethiopian pussy, was of where and when everyone was going and how, in the different destinations, they'd be treated. Meaning: would the bartenders of Sydney or Auckland overcharge them? And would the ladies of Rio part their knees? A few guys in Kfir, in Nahshon, were passing around a Spanish-Hebrew phrasebook—no entiendo? no comprendo? Por favor, hable más despacio—but Yoav said that in Rio they spoke Portuguese, which was quintessential Yoav, always stamping out the fire.

The very last days, the rift begins: from thinking about the unit, to thinking about the self, about yourself. About the resources available to you after the army. The scope of the imagination, being circumscribed by family, would reveal your family: would reveal your finances, culture, class. Menachem started flipping through Harley Davidson brochures, wondering which bike to buy with the reward his parents were giving him just for finishing his stint. Gad started drifting off to lounge under a palm and reacquaint himself with the state of international poetry. Everyone was becoming deequalized, each groping toward his individuality in a great dismemberment of a corpse—the amputation of shredded legs (Rotem's), the removal of ruptured spleens (Dror's)—and the pain Uri would come to feel would be like a phantom pain, as the spare parts of what had also been him went out stumping across the earth, or were buried alone below it.

Finally, there was another ceremony, this at the base in Eliakim, when you were reminded of what you'd been forced, or had forced yourself, to forget. When the same parents who'd said the Shalom that meant Goodbye to their boys at the Kotel now caravanned out to the grassy vale of the Galilee to say the Shalom that meant Hello, to pick their boys up and bring them home again as men—the parents too had aged in the interim.

You were reminded, by the fathers' flashy phones and the mothers' flashy jewels and especially by all the flashy Chevy Malibus they drove, of how divided everyone was, of how disparate your own brooded circumstances.

Because Uri's parents didn't make it: they couldn't. The family Dugri hadn't been present at either occasion: neither the induction nor the farewell. They never took off work. Or they'd only have taken off work for a funeral.

It was Yoav's parents, then, who offered to drive Uri home—but he refused them. Nika was out of their way and anyway, though this Uri didn't say, he didn't know whether, or what, they'd been told by their son, and it enraged him to think they might be grateful to him for whatever oblivious thing he did in that alley doorway in Jabalia. Save a guy's life and get a ride for your troubles, and maybe a roadside pita, maybe also a beer—save the gestures. He thanked them and, like the hero he was, turned them down.

Once the highway dusts settled behind them, he went out, thumb out, hitchhiking. He was picked up by an assistant to a rosh yeshivah and then by a dumptruck, which dumped him in Tel Aviv from which he took a sherut—charity be damned.

Because he was damned. In that the army, which had always purported to be so boundlessly concerned for him that he'd barely conceived ever having to outgrow it, now appeared to him spiteful, resentful, and conjugally cruel—as limiting as the dates on Shlomo "Shlo" Regev's gravemarker: (5754–5774)/ (1994–2014)—a time parenthetically tragic, whose sole legacy was an evasion, and a skillset inapplicable, even inimical, to adulthood. He'd been discharged as an expert in stealth who now to succeed had to make himself heard and seen. An expert in orienteering who now had to navigate the nettles of the occident. He was a man with a single citizenship and, discounting his Arabic, a single language, both of which were welcomed only in lands as distant from one another as the black pentagons on a white football. He was a single man who'd become singleminded about calibers and ranges, after all his juvenile interests in metal guitar and manga and capoeira and scorpions—after all the interests he'd had before his service that weren't Batya—had been decimated by the protocols and facts.

Like, the Al Ghoul is a 14.5mm rifle so accurate that if fired from Gaza can mow the lawn in Sderot, up to two kilometers away.

Like, the M113 APC Zelda has insufficient armoring against IEDs and Hashim RPGs and is, in general, an inappropriate vehicle for urban conflicts.

Don't confirm insurgent identity by uniform, confirm by gun. The enemy might copy your vest but they're carrying Kalashnikovs.

Just because you're not in a tunnel doesn't mean you're not above a tunnel, which might collapse. No tunnel's cleared until it's collapsed.

If one of the cows of the Arabushim wanders out from its pen and falls into a pit, it's better not to attempt a rescue, it's better just to shoot it.

The most dangerous spiders are the brownies and the most dangerous brownies have red or orange hourglasses on their abdomens. The yellowpatched wasp or hornet nests underground and feeds sweetly on bees. Also the human body, left alone, with no other persons, materials, or objects around—no dumbbells or doorhandles and no weapons, of course—is incapable of selfdestruction.

Sure, the body can always wait itself out, by starving or dehydration, no doubt, but assuming a certain timeframe— between a day or three, say—no human can do enough damage to himself with his own hands, with his own lonesome somatic contortions, to die. Try and hold your breath, you'll eventually, reflexively, gasp. Try and strangle yourself, just fingers choking your throat, and while you might pass out, you'll come to soon enough. There's just no way, unassisted, to commit suicide.

But then there's no way to be just a human, isolated, stripped or just stripped of contexts—because even a cell must have a floor, a ceiling, walls.

And God, don't forget God.

That Creator of all, Who's everywhere: He's everywhere at all times and even nowhere, or especially there, numinous in void. Uri had known a lot of people who'd believed that. Who'd believed that and used Him, both in and out of the army. He'd known a lot of people who'd committed suicide with God.

This was what he'd intended to bring up with the Baba Batra, the Master of the Last Gate, the Light of Porat Yosef. But once he'd finally been admitted to the rabbi's inky cramped chambers, he'd been sapped of nerve.

He was being called to account for his piety, his habits hygienic, dietary, doxological—"You pray the Shema?"

"I do," Uri said, "yes."

"Every day?"

"Every day, rabbi."

"When you go to sleep and when you wake up?"

"Yes, rabbi."

"With your strong hand covering your eyes like you're cupping a flame?"

"Covering, yes, absolutely."

"And you say it aloud so that anyone who passes your door can listen in and share in the deed, but the blessing that follows you say to yourself in a whisper?"

"In a whisper."

The rabbi growled, "Then I will tell you why you have the headaches."

"Why?"

"Because you lie to me. The headaches you have are all in your head. Tell me, where else should they be? In Tafilalt or Antwerp or Los Angeles, where? Should they be in this lamp? Or doing the Mimuna dance inside this computer? It's the truth, this pain of yours. It's the truth in pain because confined."

"Honestly, rabbi, I do pray."

"Not the Shema?"

"No."

"That's not enough for you?"

"The Shema? All it says is that God is One—it doesn't even ask for anything."

"So what then?"

"Please God don't let me die. Or do let me die. Please God for Batya Neder. I pray that I always have enough water or enough of the tablets that purify water. That I have no more freezedried goulash or freezedried schnitzel or loof. Hashem, I pray, no more dreams."

"Amen."

"But, rabbi, what do they mean?"

"The dreams? What don't they mean? Like every election has its scandal, every dream has its nonsense. This is why no dream is ever completely fulfilled."

"So trying to explain them is futile?"

"Like dreaming that your dream is being interpreted. My beard is the interpretation."

Uri fidgeted, the rabbi picked at his beard. "Consider the difference," he said, "between trials and tests—what's your name again?"

"Uri."

"The warrior, kindled by God—it's up to you, Uri, to distinguish between them."

"Between what?"

"There are trials of faith, given directly by God. Like how God told Abraham to leave his land and kill his own son and how because Abraham set out to do what he was told, we became the chosen and an angel was sent at the last moment to grab the blade away."

"And what's the other kind?"

"Tests that are temptations, tricks, deceptions. Which are the work of women, serpents, and brothers."

"All of them together?"

"Who offered Adam the fruit? A woman, Eve. And who offered the fruit to Eve? The serpent, Satan. Cain murders Abel and then, given the chance to admit his guilt, decides to lie, like you've lied. And this is just one family."

"You're saying it's like my family?"

"I'm saying that in life, it's most important to understand what is being judged. And what is the intention."

"I don't understand."

"Your loyalty is being judged."

"How? Because I'm so"—and hesitated, and then said it—"fucked up?"

"No," the rabbi said, "nothing to do with fucked up."

"Then why?"

"Because the army might not be over. Because the army might never be over. You're being challenged, as to whether you believe that. Or else it's all just a ploy and you're being tricked into believing you were discharged."

"It is? I wasn't?"

"No, Uri—because you can't stop being a soldier, just like you can't stop being a Jew. They're both permanent conditions, for life. This is the position of the State of Israel. You were born a soldier, because you were born a Jew, and if you weren't given an Uzi at your bris it was only because the government won't issue them to anyone not old enough to handle the commitment. To handle the burden. To join the army is to accept who you are. To formally accept it. And the age requirements and set period of service are just traditions—bureaucracy."

"So I'm still serving—that's what you mean? And you don't mean like in the reserves?"

"At age 13, you were called to the Torah to become a bar mitzvah—a son of the commandments?"

"Of course."

"Of course—you know this, you remember. But did you know that at age 18, you were called to become another thing, a bar pekudah—a son of the commands?"

"I didn't."

"Tell me, bar pekudah, after you became a bar mitzvah and read from the Torah—maybe had a little party, maybe had a little cake—did you stop being a Jew?"

"Of course not."

"Of course not. So then why, after the army asks you to leave, do you stop being a soldier?"

"I'm not sure."

"It's only after the army asks you to leave that you start—because it's only after that you're prepared, with a feeling for the graveness of the duty."

The Baba Batra's phone illumined and vibrated across his desk to a trancehop ringtone and he leaned to mute it, put a palm to Uri's forehead, blessed him.

Whiteclad flunkies ushered Uri out and down the halls past the expectant infertile and abiding cancered and all the crutches and casts of the waylaid maimed, who reached out to touch the hem of his garment.

✿

Yoav was moving. Between Harlem and the Village, Staten Island and the Bronx.

He was trucking across the Verrazano, the Throggs Neck, the George Washington, or coming through the Lincoln Tunnel (because 4, 5, and 6 axle trucks were prohibited from using the Holland), heading to Jersey—to load a whole apartment into the hold of a 12 footer, to unload all the foamcushioned contents of a brownstone packed inside a 21 footer. In a tractortrailer towing an entire office, an entire office building. In a pickup droppingoff potted rubbertrees and sacks of mulch. In a cargo van containing chandeliers for a Midtown penthouse and Hamptons summer bicycles.

The traffic flowed like the rivers: sometimes south, sometimes north, and sometimes in both directions simultaneously.

Which was sometimes not at all.

A group of guys go out hard, swarming the houses of strangers, taking the furniture apart, taking the furniture away, breaking shit by accident, and not by accident, committing petty theft by accident, and not by accident or always petty, fucking up the linoleums, leaving everything empty, leaving everything a mess—who would've guessed that the army had been training him for moving?

Which meant that moving was what—a duty? A calling? A job? Another occupation?

Whatever it was, it had to feel compulsory.

Meals were rationed (he rationed them), launderings were regulated (he regulated them). Days were scheduled into hours, each hour had its task, each task had its coordinate. This was how he protected himself. This, to him, was normal.

The last of the month and the first of the month were the busiest, and the busiest season, summer's encroachment on fall. Each move was like a mission: each morning he'd start somewhere new, each evening he'd end up somewhere else, and between the two indefinites just sweat—just sweat and repetition.

Ruth (for the first two weeks) or Paul Gall (thereafter) would call with orders to report to an address off Times Square, but then the day would close with Wall Street.

It was a Wednesday, his second Wednesday, that marked the date: he'd been moving now for as long as his war had lasted—for longer. His weapons were the harness and dolly, his uniform a blue zipup onesie, and either this was David's error, or Ruth's, or the manufacturer's, but above the King's Moving diadem, the embroidery read: YO AV.

He finally got paid after about a month—a period of time known to Israelis and only the closest of foreign allies as half a visa—half a US B-2 visitors visa, whose reverse was printed with the following message: PERSON IDENTIFIED BY THIS CARD IS NOT AUTHORIZED TO WORK IN THE UNITED STATES.

Neither was he authorized to operate a vehicle, let alone one of the class 4, 5, or 6 commercial vehicles King's Moving was using, so sometimes this guy called Jon was at the wheel, and at other times this guy called Leland.

Yoav was getting paid to get to know the city. At least well enough to know that, even with his expenses taken care of, his rate was criminal. $10/hour. Cash.

The guys—the personnel he worked with, all guys—changed, nearly as often as the customers. So many names came at him, so many handshakes callused and chapped. It was difficult to determine the ranks, especially because he was family: the movers were below the drivers were below the office staff, whose chain of command went Paul Gall, Ruth, David . . . or Ruth, Paul Gall, David . . . or Paul Gall, David, Ruth—depending on weekday, weekend, time of day, type of task, and mood. Above everyone, though, was the customer, the King of King's who was also the adversary. Ruth's life was dealing with their sniping, and with the men: the men who trashed the kitchenette, the men who trashed the women's bathroom, her bathroom, the men from Xerox and Time Warner. She handled the insurance claims, made change for the vendingmachines, and was always taking Yoav's temperature: "If you're feeling up to it this weekend, I'm trying to get David to take us applepicking by the Delaware."

Paul Gall, that pursy bobbleheaded ex-Yugo from Belgrade, shambled around in a nappy sheening gemdealer's kaftan only because it had the greatest number of pockets for his Crown Royal flasks and Kools. He specialized in scheduling: "Your cousin, he's been like my brother, but cross me and I'll cut your shifts, cross me again and I'll cut you down to storage." Inside the office, because smoking was banned, he sucked on a tire gauge and was always cracking his molars. His son, Tom Gall, did client liaison, new business recruitment, and marketing/PR,

and had arrogated to himself over a dozen VP titles he'd em-
bossed onto businesscards at his own expense, so there wasn't
any need to inform his father, or David, or Ruth: he only handed
the cards out to women he wanted to impress, women who'd
recently immigrated. He'd been in the armed forces too, but the
US armed forces, the USCG, stationed off Cape May, the Jersey
Shore theater: "But I was also in the Gulf, securing the shipping-
routes and ports, rebuoying the Tigris and Euphrates, making
sure we got the crude and you small countries had the big guns
behind you." Gyorgi had worked as a mover until he'd touched a
female minor who'd clerked at a gypsum sheather in Paterson,
served most of a lenient sentence, and was now confined behind
a storage cage to be more findable by his parole officer. Tinks
had a mohawk, a nose ring, a tattoo on one hand, Itch, another
on the other, Scratch. He was in noise bands, did puppetry with
scrap aluminum, and made promises, though as of yet hadn't
delivered on any, to modernize the computer systems at King's
Moving, and develop its presence online. Ronaldo Rodriguez,
AKA Ronriguez, AKA Godriguez, AKA Burrito Ron, earned the
last of his nicknames pioneering the technique of taking a customer's odd loose possessions and rolling them up in a rug for
efficiency of transport. He was a squat wideassed low center of
gravity surmounted by a slick pubic moustache. Malcolm C,
alias Talcum X, powdered his pits to stay dry and his hands to
improve his grip. He was bullet bald and jacked, with two additional adductor muscles found in only .006% of the population.

Before jobs, or on breaks during jobs, or between jobs, some
guy would go out for tacos and some guy would go out for subs
and then another guy would break away for a cigpack or sixpack
he'd never share, and that was acceptable, no one was whining.

It was acceptable for a worker to only take care of himself. Yoav would do a full day with a guy who'd tell him every detail about fucking his wife, how he fucked her, how she came, how he came wicked buckets, and then he'd just—evaporate: Yoav would never work with him again, no one would ever mention him, no one would even remember. "Kwanye K." Kwame, "Daddy" Mackenson, Nelson, that Guy Without A Lip, this guy from maybe but maybe not Paraguay, they called him Paragay—it was Yoav's flaw to regard their transience, and the transience of institutional memory, as rude, because the truth was, it was life.

In this inexperience of his, in his sensitivities, Yoav resembled his customers—white kids even if they weren't white kids— much more than he resembled his coworkers. Initial jobs had him in and out of the city, moving the arrivals in for school, be- cause school was back in session, moving the departures out, new grads returning to parental houses, or to outerborough apartments the size of cubicles, rooms with the squarefootage of diplomas, rooms as costly as diplomas. Yoav wasn't sure how to take them, the customers who shared his age, whether as adults or as children. If in America they were both then he was neither.

They lived without elevators, on top floors, down narrow halls, under low ceilings. Studios listed as one bedrooms, though the kitchens and bedrooms were contiguous, one bed- rooms rented as twos, illegally rented, because bedroom num- ber two had no window.

Their bongs would be left out in the open. Their weed was in the drawer with the checkbook and diverse colors and shapes of pills.

They'd use their own boxes, flyblown, loosebottomed, soggy from the dumpsters. They'd rumple their soiled linens into flimsy tieless garbagebags that at the moment of lifting would tear and crusty underthings would drift down to the sidewalk like rusty leaves.

Some kids would try to carry their own weight and do their own binning, acting like they were workers themselves—like they were used to this type of labor, or like it was fitness to them, or fun, to slum and rip a hand bloody on a crate, drop a footlocker on a foot. The kid, a college blond, must've been ashamed of being wealthy, or of not being as wealthy as his parents, who were paying for the move, just like they'd paid for all of his apartments. He was writhing on the floor, cradling his foot and unable to rise. Tom Gall called an ambulance and Talc and Ronriguez loaded the kid onto a handtruck and stretchered him down. The kid himself called his father who now had to taxi over from his investment firm in Manhattan to supervise the movers—to supervise them at both move locations—the father sitting on the windowsill typing on his laptop in Greenpoint and then, across the toxic creek in Long Island City, restless atop the radiator and receiving an update from the kid's mother, who'd met their son at the NYU ER, where he was being treated for fractured pride and three broken toes.

Other kids at least admitted their ineptitude, particularly in situations in which new furniture was due to be delivered to their new apartments—they'd beg for help with its assembly, and when there wasn't an immediate next job, sometimes, for extra cash, Yoav would stay, sometimes along with a Brazilian named Grio, and the two would attempt to follow the incoherent instructions in a language that neither spoke, that no one spoke: "Affit joint A to peg B use 4 rings twice. Repeat the peg again with gluer unincluded." Male customers would have to pay more for this. The ladies paid less, though they often opted to solicit the help of the furniture deliverers themselves and, anyway, if the ladies were in any manner construable as cute, or sexually acquiescent in the dimples, Grio, sleazily gallant, would refuse his fee, which meant that Yoav had to refuse his too, and be called a Jew for doing so begrudgingly, as he'd leave the customer to the Brazilian's devices, to his pliers and dowels and charms.

It unnerved, that after a move was over, the crew would never leave together: after they split the tip, they split up into the hordes, dispersing their creaturely reeks among the harried commuters.

Yoav wasn't sure what permissions he had—to ask a ride from his coworkers, even just to ask directions—and so he'd be left on his own standing in twilight trying to figure out what corner he was on and how he was going to get out of there.

On foot, because the buses were still incomprehensible to him, and as for the trains, they were underground, and he'd had enough of tunnels.

———

A pregnant couple transitioning from a single room situation to an extra room situation . . . a pair of grown siblings who'd already evacuated their geriatric parents into assistedliving from out of the classic 6 condo they were looting . . .

The customers: they'd lead the way in a taxi up front and the moving truck, a boxtruck or tractortrailer, would follow just behind—taking the transverse through the Park, crosstown. From where the sun rises on the Upper East, to where it sets on the Upper West. No matter who drove or rode, Yoav would be sitting bitch. In the middle.

This was always the fragile time, the breakable time, the time of slip and slide and jostle. The ride between the old apartment already moved out, and the new apartment not yet moved into, during which life itself would come to seem like just another vehicle set in motion between unrelated emptinesses. For a moment, your burdens were suspended. For a certain span of mileage, you were weightless, you were free.

This was Yoav's passage, his reprieve: sitting high above a taxi, its windows steamed from grievance, and feeling the rumbling coming up from below, springs poking his balls through the vinyl, stickshift rattling between his legs.

Each move had its own logistics, each party to a move its own subterfuges. Because the customers would misrepresent their possessions on the online form, Ruth would have to call and followup: buildings vet prospective tenants, movers vet prospective loads. Prewar or Postwar were no indications, the preferred criterion was: Yes Elevator, No Elevator. All planning proceeded from there: what floor, the number of flights of stairs, the number of stairs per flight, the number of rooms (incl. attic, incl. basement).

The desire to get finished earlier vs. the desire to drag a job out, because the crews got paid for their time. The desire to take a break vs. the desire to finish earlier, because the crews didn't get paid for their breaks. Whether to work by the room or by item size. Whether to work by the room as arranged at move out or as it would be arranged at move in. Load the big stuff first, to maximize truckspace (crew philosophy). Load the big stuff last, to waste truckspace but require more trips, which meant more time, maximizing profit (philosophy of Paul Gall).

Because packing was distinct from moving, both in terms of

expertise and pricing structure, the chief distinction to be found amongst the customers wasn't related to anything indelible like melanin or age, but to money—between those who'd packed themselves and those who hadn't. Or between those who were present at their moves and those rich enough to be moved while away on vacation. Yoav and the others would storm up to their residential fortresses that were like something out of some fantastic antique duchy of Middle Europe: blocksize, gated, the turrets set with spikes, the bastions lacking only cannon. The doorman, dressed like a general, wouldn't want them in the lobby. The super, dressed like his adjutant, wouldn't want them in the halls. Elevator policy was enforced, one was for service, the other for the served. Each to their own capacities. The movers had to wear sticker IDs that read Contractor. They had to read a screen and click Agree. They were warned, they were being watched, listened to, background-checked, and screened for cimices, termites, roaches, warrants, priors. The patrols weren't armed by building ownership or management, but by the city, because they were cops, just offduty. Rules included no cursing and keep your pants up at your fucking waists and don't take your motherfucking shirts off. Finally, they'd be let into an apartment, and everything would just be out, immaculately staged and dusted. Nothing would be boxed. Nothing would even be labeled. The movers would take it slow. They'd drive slow. They'd unload slow and make their own decisions. Slow. They'd sit around after, atop corpulent flatulent shrinkwrapped settees, waiting on Tinks, who'd once spent all of a paid weekend getting certified to move fine art and pianos. Someone would thump that pretty shaky on the stairs theme from the Moonlight Sonata. Someone had to argue that the sky was a lake and so the stars just reflections, which meant the painting was hanging upsidedown.

If the customer was present, odds were they'd turn out to be customers—a couple. Which meant friction. What you did was, you instructed one member of the couple to stay at the old unit and the other member to wait at the new. This tamped down dissension. Still, typically what you'd get would be one member of the couple at the old unit able to be calm and without opinion, only because there'd always be that other member at the new unit yelling at you about vase placement, about what the hell were you doing taking up that crevice with that deflowered vase, and what shocked Yoav was that every couple he'd jobbed for had evinced this divide—straight or gay, irrespective of gender, there was always a leader, a commander, as implacable as an apartment's dimensions, or a circuitbreaker impeding at midwall. The low leather suspended from tubular metal futons had to go across from each other and perpendicular to the recliner, the workbenchlike table had to be set with a chair at each extremity and disposited flush with the counter partiwalling the kitchen, and the Shaker dresser that Yoav noted was missing two drawerhandles prior to transport was to be situated, regardless of all physical limitations, in the bedroom athwart the bed, the customer having calculated, or having sworn that they'd calculated, the minimum clearance by which an open drawer wouldn't bump an open door. If you couldn't angle a table you had to amputate its limbs and hump the rest across the banisters. If you couldn't get a dresser through the door just by taping its drawers you had to remove the drawers and then, in turning, let the hollows accommodate the knob. If the argument was with you, give in. If the argument was within the couple, stay out of it. Customers fought, as you labored, on their own time. And the nastier the fight, the nicer the tip.

Another thing about couples: they tended to move in together (hiring one crew for both members), but move out separately (hiring one crew for each member)—the lesson being that while making a life together took more toil, unmaking that life took more cash.

Ruth would put it differently, while giving estimates: if you try to save time, you'll just wind up getting charged for an additional vehicle plus tolls.

Yoav once moved a couple from their separate apartments in Chelsea and Murray Hill to a loftbuilding still being refurbished in Astoria. The couple had doubles of everything, but didn't want to get rid of the excess, and definitely didn't want the movers to do the ridding for them, so: four bedstands, two beds. The building had once been a factory for coffins. The elevator was for freight and operated by a crank you tugged with your hand not like you were directing it up or down but like you were directly cranking its engine or pulleying. Eighth floor. The couple was in a fit. They were insisting they'd signed a contract for 8G, but the broker or building rep kept saying they hadn't and that 8H was "fundamentally the same unit: same size, same layout, same view."

The couple didn't agree: 8H had a tinier laundrynook, the tinier laundrynook was adjacent to the kitchen, and the windows faced airshaft, not street.

The broker was a freckled redhead in a baggy suit and an exterminator's cologne.

Yoav and Tinks and Mark from Philly who was Tinks' current roommate and this weakling asthmatic guy with a do-rag, braces, and a lanyarded inhaler who called himself D'Bruce and never showed for work again, continued to unload in the hall, as the couple demanded to be let into 8G to compare, but the broker didn't have the key. The man called the management company, the woman slit tape and mauled cardboard in search of their contract, which they'd packed.

Yoav never found out how it all got resolved, after the couple signed for Leland and returned the clipboard and pen, which the broker was claiming was his pen, he was yelling about how they couldn't leave, they couldn't obstruct the exits, "my pen," and Leland exited, shrugging.

The couple's stuff was left heaped in the hall: suitcases, crates, a shrieking sawdusted cage of albino mice.

Gowanus, this other couple that lived together was no longer together—meaning they no longer shared the bedroom but shared the rest. Sheets and blankets had been folded on the gashed velvet of a loveseat. The couple was on the floor, still snatching at paperbacks, reacquiring their libraries, haggling over LPs and a tattered poster of sunflowers not flirtatiously but with passion, their feud degenerating from the issue of what was whose before the merger to what should or could be whose if certain trades or admissions of guilt or sincere psychologically reparative apologies were tendered. Ronriguez was still out with the truck, doubleparked between a driveway and a hydrant. Talc took a phonecall and because it was about his landscaping business, or the landscaping business he'd be founding the moment any bank approved him for a loan, he took it outside, and came back waving a $120 ticket.

The couple's final disagreement—after Jon insisted their

moves had to happen today—was over the order of the moving: who'd vacate the premises first.

The woman said, "Him first," but the man said, "You're going to Connecticut, I'm just down the block," and the woman said, "Shouldn't keep your new slut waiting," and the man said, "Couldn't stop banging your boss," and the woman said, "Whoever cheated first, moves first."

"If you keep on like this," Tinks said, "we're going to have to send Yo uptown to get us one of them UN negotiators."

After returning from moving the man, Talc and Ronriguez were cut loose because of conflicts: Talc had to testdrive some preowned hedgers, edgers, and pruners, Ronriguez had his second job at a carwash. The woman was sobbing.

Her stuff was loaded and the sun was low in the clouds and Connecticut, like childhood, just kept getting farther.

"We're ready," Jon said, "whenever you are," but the woman just sat on the stoop with her totebag open in her lap for her tears.

"I'm not going—I'm crashing at a friend's—tell my Dad—or I told him already but still," she said, "I was supposed to get my friend's keys, but then she was called into a meeting and said not to come to the office, she'd come to me, when she's out of the meeting, or if it goes late I'm supposed to be in touch with her boyfriend, or not her boyfriend but this guy she's, who works at the climbingwall restaurant, she met him online, and at my Dad's house everything can go in the basement except my lilies, which he's going to have to water."

"Word."

Jon's phone calculated the route with such immediacy, it was as if they didn't have to drive it, the roads had already driven themselves.

New Canaan—1010 WINS here, even the GPS here, was too loud, so Jon turned them down, and Tinks had stopped talking, about girls of his who'd OD'd, or noosed themselves, or slashed their wrists wrongly across and not lengthwise, and this festival of documentaries he was going to, or had a documentary he'd made in competition in.

The house glowed like a bulb from out of the dark socket of culdesac. Two figures flustered like moths: the wife trim and grinning with hair flapping just past her ears, the husband bloated with round thick architect's glasses that, because he wasn't an architect, his wife must've picked.

"I can't thank you enough," she said and shook Jon's hand. "I'm the stepmother."

The husband was intent on pitching in, but she wouldn't let him, and told Jon not to let him, so Jon told him he'd best be of help guarding the truck, to ensure that nothing was taken, and they left the man standing curbside redundant and sullen, in a neighborhood that never took, because there was nothing it didn't already own.

After Jon, Yoav, and Tinks had stoked the basement, the wife invited them to stay—there was still stirfry leftover from supper and the movers gathered around the table as she warmed it in a pan on the stove. The microwave heated unevenly and wasn't healthy. Stirfry with white meat, mixed veggies. The husband was into stocks. The wife had retired as a speechlanguage pathologist. They'd talk about anything not to talk about their girl. For example, the rain (how bad would it be?). For example, Yoav's origins (the Middle East?).

"Israel," Yoav said.

Tinks said, "And I'm from Atlanta."

The wife said, "George."

The husband was picking at the triveted pan. "What?"

"You already ate supper."

"But I'm hungry."

The wife got him a fork. "At least don't use your nasty hands—I bet they don't eat like that in Israel."

Tinks said, "Suburban Atlanta."

The wife said, "George."

"What, darling?"

"Not straight from the pan," and then she served her husband a miserable portion. "The boy said he's from Israel."

The husband bowed his head and bit into a babycorn.

"That food's so delicious," the wife went on. "The hummus—and the nuggets? What are they called? Don't tell me—I'll get it. You know, I never knew until there was this cooking event at the church that the nuggets were just made from the same thing the hummus is—the beans? Barganzos?"

The husband got up, went to a cabinet for glasses and wine. "Anyone?"

The wife said, "Enough red. White."

Tinks said, "Please."

Jon said, "We're OK. I'm driving."

The husband said, "Red."

The wife said, "You've got gout."

The husband said, "And you've got your sleeve in the soysauce."

The wife got up, rinsed her sleeve in the sink. "So Israel—I'd love to have gone, but unfortunately."

The husband said, "Strong pharma in that country of yours. Tech sector too. Energy's developing. You in with any funds?"

"I'd love to have gone, but George couldn't."

"Not true." The husband drained the bottle in his glass.

The wife said, "The church was having this tour, Red Sea, Dead Sea, Nazareth, Jerusalem. But George didn't feel up to it, not with his ankle. All those stairs out of stone. All those quaint winding streets."

The husband forked at Yoav, "That's what it's like, isn't it?"

Yoav said, "In Jerusalem the most."

The wife said, "That's what it said in the pamphlet: follow in the footsteps of Jesus—but it didn't say how many steps."

"Outside Jerusalem, it very modern."

"We went into Manhattan to visit—we went to a matinee of *The Lion King*, just this past Labor Day weekend, and George could barely make it the two avenue blocks back to the garage."

Coming out of Connecticut, it was raining moonless and the roads were slick—Jon remaining vigilant about the driveways, which were hidden like the mouths to caves by bush and shrub, the burrowed hibernacles of affluence.

The only voice in the truck was machinic, robotic—the GPS giving directions and constantly rerouting, Thruway to the Expressway rerouting, until the Major Deegan slowed, then stopped. The access road was better.

And then it might've been Woodlawn, because there were woods, out of which scampered a child, because a deer can still be a child, frozen knockkneed atop the dotted line, and Jon stomped the brake and turned into the skid, tossing them all forward into the impact. Tinks bucked and Yoav reached out to keep from hitting the dash and then—pressured in his chest—

was wrenched back by his seatbelt, pinching him like the strap of a ghost rifle.

The truck was slung across an intersection, cab and trailer splayed like clockhands. They might also have been hit from the rear. The most vexing thing about a sizable vehicle is that you can't keep track of most of it. You're like an enormous metal animal that doesn't know it's picked up an enormous metal tick, until the tick explodes. Out the truck's windows, the houses went rubbling away into darkness and a fog swirled up with the stench of scorched rubber. The wind strewed trash across the street, spooked trashbags out of their mounds into the air. Yoav kept checking the mirrors. He didn't know where the shooting was coming from. They were pinned. The vehicle shook and the radiophone was blaring. He ducked but swiveled around, as the shooting kept coming in bursts from 10 o'clock and 2 o'clock and down on the roof like rain. Then he realized, the doors were open and he was alone. You weren't supposed to get out of the vehicle, but wherever the others were, they were out of the vehicle. Yoav thought that maybe he was the driver now. He thought that maybe if he'd honk too the rest of the crew would return and not just strand him. The fire sprayed and did not discriminate. You killed the windows to kill the buildings. You killed the corner buildings to kill the streets. He sat, immobilized, with a motor's buzz under the hood of his ears, and the glint of glass like life in his eye, like some star, to take direction from until its fading. Someone was approaching, blood spurting from the nose like a siren. You weren't supposed to get out of the vehicle, and yet here he was, getting dragged out. He was being shoved toward the trees.

"Go," Jon yelled, "get out of here."

Whatever Yoav said was Hebrew.

"You're in the Bronx," Jon yelled, "you understand me? The Bronx? Take a taxi, a car service. Have them take you home."

Yoav again, in crunched Hebrew.

"Yo, we had an accident, the police are going to come, they're going to bring us in, and you're working without papers, you're illegal, goddamnit, so make yourself scarce—that's an order."

Tinks was behind the truck, trying to open the door, any of the doors, of the yellow SUV whose grille was all up in the truck's hitch totaled. He was flopped across the seats slapping the driver awake, as Yoav staggered past.

At the bottom of a pothole crater a child animal howled.

It was only when Yoav held a wad of bills in his hand and was being waved toward the trees that he understood this wasn't Gaza.

It was cold and wet and the grasses were endless. He made his way around the rolls of razorwire around a cemetery. The black stones became black houses, aerialed projects. All the taxis that passed were off for the night, so were now just the cars of drivers heading to their cable packages and their wives, and none were stopping or even slowing.

He chased after a bus, which lit the way to the subway, which was elevated here. And Yoav, soaked to his purpose, ascended the platform and rode through the sky, until he was swallowed down into the guts.

———

His chest was aching for a while after, though that could've been from an earlier wound or the suffocating emptiness of time. The days were swelling inside him, the offdays, the Tues, the Wed, the Thurs. Midweek. Midmonth. Days idling. Days chained together and towed into sleeplessness swinging and rattling.

He tried requesting extra jobs, but with Talc having to finance his landscaping, and Ronriguez having to refinance his third baby, Paul Gall was prioritizing their overtime. He took the issue up with Ruth, who told him to chill like the weather, check out a museum, a park, a girl, all of which were free and not only in Manhattan.

In Manhattan, he found himself a block from his cousin's and called and David picked up and said that if Yoav was just downstairs then Yoav must be in Canada, because David was in Ontario pricing a conveyor system.

Yoav wondered what'd happen if he'd just casually show up to a job another crew was slotted for, but he couldn't find the address. It was like 315 Broad had been moved so thoroughly, there wasn't even a vacant lot—like 315 had ceased to be a number.

He wasn't used to making decisions like this, he wasn't able to choose, and not just because of the army. The notion of being free to do whatever you wanted, virtually whenever you wanted, had been so alien to the family Matzav, it was like having a relative you hadn't been in contact with for such an immensity of time that you were doubting his existence, until out of nowhere you were forced together and thrust into recognizance.

The only choices Yoav was capable of making, then, were minor, befitting his rank: he, who'd always shaved his head, or let Reuven do it for him, was now growing it out into a patchy coronation. He was realizing that he'd never liked beer, he liked rum. He still wasn't sure about cigs, though, which meant he was addicted. Flossing didn't make him a fag. From now on he'd wear boxers, not even boxerbriefs, and briefs never again. His socks wouldn't be the tall tubes anymore but the shorties. He'd turned to reading, and didn't care that Gad, who read English but swore Hemingway was better in Hebrew, and Kosta, who only read articles glamorizing the Shabak and Mossad, would've heaved him to the latrines for the sites he now perused—sites on Israeli history, the reconstruction of Salah al-Din Road, and FAQs about how to be an actor. He kept the TV tuned to topical series and serious cinema and drew his own conclusions: his tastes could be improved. And even certain thoughts—not overtly political but just the thoughts or intimations or taints of impatience that might come from being stuck in line behind a grubby slow salaaming human of another race who kept changing his mind about his Power-ball digits at the deli—he'd have to break with those thoughts. He couldn't stay in America without breaking those thoughts and dealing with the guilt.

He stopped answering his phone (his Israeli phone, not the American phone David had given him), and returned its calls (but only his mother called his Israeli phone) only when he was sure his mother was unavailable. But if she ever tried him on the American phone—Yoav had no clue how she'd gotten that (917), whether from him in a slip, or she'd extorted it from David—he'd pick up, he'd have to, because he'd be curious, and she'd greet him by saying, "You got fired?"

He had to account for his time, and tell her where he'd vis-ited and with whom, and such was her appetite—or his solitude and the greed of her pauses—that he lied: "I've been going to shows."

"What shows?"

"Good shows, at the Broadway theater, the one about the lion, and then the other one"—he tried to recall the ads—"about the Arab kid with the genie."

"You made friends with David's daughter?"

"Tammy—she's very smart, a nonprofit."

"What?"

"A nonprofit."

Which he said in English, though he was sure his mother didn't know what that was, though he wasn't sure he knew either

When he asked to speak to his father, her answer was: "You're not the only one who works."

He stopped replying to email, because all his former squadmates' lives suddenly seemed so frivolous, irresponsible: Iddo was surfing? Let him surf. Nachum adopted a kangaroo? May he elope with a koala. Pinchas had been fined for camping in the forest, or making a bonfire in the forest, fined and then arrested. Gershon had been with a whore in Nepal and now had a wart on his scrotum.

"And guess whose face the wart resembles?"

He was being chatted—by Eli, by Sami.

"Yoavik—you there? You online?"

As for the concerns about Uri—there were counselors for that. There were huckster wonderworkers in white hazmat suits and yarmulkes.

Yoav had come to regard, he'd come to resent, all this contact as control. All these transmissions sent through the air, these neuroses beamed, dread streamed in on the rays—from his family's phone greased up with oliveoil in the kitchen in Bat

Yam, from his squadmates' dented laptops filching wifi out on the patios of tropical cafés, and even from the mouths of the Chabad Hasidim who'd accost him in the flesh on Eastern Parkway.

There were two of them, this one dayoff, both as young as he was in the face, but their bellies made them seem older. Well fed and defanged, they seemed friendlier than Hasidim in Israel. But they couldn't have been, there shouldn't have been any differences between them. The point of being a Hasid was to be the same in every country, in every age. Still, this was a pair of Americans, soft and throbbing with jollity. They'd thrived on the luxury of their exoticism, the luxury of their otherness.

They proffered tallis and tefillin while exhorting in their stilted archaic tongue: "Bist du a yid? Du davenst?"

Yoav ignored them, but they shimmied up to either side of him, pleading in corrupt Jurassic Hebrew: "Thou art Jewish—Israeli—thou must be."

"Get a job," Yoav said.

"Pray at our shul."

"Blow me," he said, but in a slang that wouldn't be understood.

He'd miscalculated, apparently: by thinking that to leave Israel he could avoid Israel, could evade the Jews, the news—by thinking, like nearly all the customers he'd moved, that just by changing the walls around him he'd be changed within, as if all that junk that'd been pumped into his head would come tumbling out in the transit. He'd underestimated the methods, the retention initiatives, the stoploss techniques. He hadn't been counting on his squadmates to already be sending up their flares, summoning him back if not to the homefront then to his duty. Telling him what his debt was, telling him what he owed.

Whatever the army paid out to the disabled or bereaved. If only they'd accept his dollars in lieu of his presence, in lieu of his blood.

It was the holidays.

Paul Gall knew not to put Yoav on the schedule and Yoav knew not to balk. He was ashamed, though, because all throughout the three days he was missing—a stretch that might've meant six shifts, of 12, 13, even 14 jobs—he should've been begging the forgiveness of his God, but all he was occupied with was the income he was losing.

He couldn't not accept David's invitation to synagogue, to temple—showing up for Rosh Hashanah in a Champion sweatshirt and the only Levi's he had unstained.

For Yom Kippur, David insisted on putting him into a vintage polyblend suit pullulating with pleats and lapels like the wings of angels, so stiff with starch it felt like he'd crack it every time he sat and stood and genuflected in that stale churchy spanse, as the congregation wheezed hosannas in cumbrous English.

In the midst of the service, David leaned over and murmured worshipfully, "Don't forget it—I used to wear a 32 waist."

The tongue was sour from fasting, the walk uptown was slow.

David lived in a massive, stolid, brutalist block, his bachelorized co-op a strip of three units that'd been joined, or that were supposed to have been joined, in a renovation he'd left incomplete—it'd left him jaded. Two of the units—inaccessible, inhospitable, littered with the cardboard cartons from David's online impulse purchases that he never was able to bring himself to recycle—surrounded what amounted to a dismal sunken den of other people's furniture atop musty Persian rugs and loosetacked scuffed parquet infringing on a kitchen island set with sharp stools and vapid cabinetry and pristine unused appliances.

There was a slidingdoor that gave out onto a balcony of flaking masonry over hansoms and monuments to dead generals, but it was jammed.

Three women, subcontracted from an employee of the office, comprised the evening's help. They stood prim and prepared to greet in white smocks crested with the emblem of the Trump International and David, unsure as to which was Grio's mother, which was Grio's sister, and which was Grio's sister in law, just said, "You're all so youthful, I can't tell which is which."

The down the hall neighbors, the co-op secretary, the temple treasurer—David, famished for affection, hugged each between swallowing cherry blintzes.

Ruth, who couldn't be a guest without becoming a host, couldn't relax—she supervised. There weren't enough trays or just too many of veg, too few of fruit. They weren't being refreshed or unwrapped of their cling quite fast enough. The dips were being spread around and what'd been tidy scoops of overmayoed tuna and eggsalad fell into each other, became slurried.

Yoav was in a corner and deep into his bagels, beyond the initial satiation phase and immersed now in an intricate assembly: laying slabs of tomato, onion, lox. He'd commandeered his own personal twoliter of whatever Coke was left. Coke Zero. At least he wasn't drinking straight from it.

And then she was next to him, waving a cup. A woman whose

pursed posed face plumped chubbier and younger with each photo of her down the hall. Yoav poured her out some foam and as the fizzing subsided she stepped closer and he trickled in some soda. David, from across the room, gave a stupid thumbs up.

"That for me or you?" she said.

"Soda for you."

"I meant the—forget it. I'm Tammy. Your cousin? Second cousin once removed?"

Yoav furrowed like he was figuring it out, hoping to confirm her.

She picked up a napkin. "Not trying to be awkward, but—creamcheese?"

Yoav muffled whatever he was saying by wiping knuckles across his lips.

"That's it, all gone. You've got it."

She'd made a fist around the napkin. "How's that for an icebreaker?" And now chucked it to a shelf. "Don't you just hate these?"

"What you hate?"

"What do I? A ton of shelf with no books. Or nothing you'd ever read. And all this weird decor crap that doesn't have any function, just sits there. These large wooden apples, like if I wanted an apple, I'd definitely want one way too large to bite into and anyway made out of maple. Or, like, here's an innovation, let's not have any plants, because plants require effort, let's just have a chintzy dish in the shape of a leaf. What's it filled with? Rainbow gravel. I wonder what poor fuck's house he took that out of? Did he just take the dish or did it come with the gravel?"

"What poor fuck?"

Tammy took a sip and stifled a belch. "Because I can't imagine him buying gravel."

"What you have in your house?"

"Driving to the store, finding parking—does he even bother to feed the meter? Going inside and buying gravel."

"In what neighborhood you live?"

Tammy gulped down her cup. "I like the suit."

She reached between the wooden apples for the scotch, turned the labels to get the best or just the aged of the bottles, poured and cheersed him, "To the Jews."

The sad nonclink of plastics.

"It's sad," she said.

"What?"

"Everything—it's desperate. Me coming like this. Coming late and leaving early. I give him once a year."

"Always a holiday?"

Tammy poured refills. "Or sometimes I go to the dinner thing with the Pharaoh and the matzah."

"Pesach."

"I give him once a year. But for her it's a fulltime job, like literally."

"Who?"

"Her," and Tammy dipped her cup toward Ruth and said, "Ruth. You know what she told me? That she comes to this stuff because she knows I won't. All she can think about, she says, is how depressed he gets if I don't show. How fucked is that? She's not the office manager, she's the life manager. Pretends that she's my mom. Pretends that she's his wife. Sits around all

week waiting for my prick father to make plans for the weekend and then, because he never does, she knits, she phones for
Thai."

Yoav nodded toward David, "Maybe he now just a friend?"

"Maybe he now can go fuck himself—what kind of friend is
that? She helps him through his heart thing, he barely calls her
through her breast cancer. She remembers his birthday, she
remembers my birthday, meanwhile he forgets hers and misses
her graduation after she went out and got that master's in admin
for him. He never even went to a single one of her tapdance
recitals. That's what she said. But then he just stops by Hoboken without any warning and tries to fuck her, and the worst of
it is, she was telling me, that since his heart he can't even get it
up, and she tells me this not like she's slagging on him but like
she's assuming I know this already or want to know, and she
wants to assure me it's OK by her, she's coping with it."

"This happens?"

"Typical employer/employee relationship. And according to
her, my mother's the meddler."

"And what you are?

"About to bounce."

Ruth was standing between them and said, "I'm not inter-
rupting but Yoav, dear, would you mind folding up the chairs?"

Tammy went to get her coat and huddled in it against her
father on the sofa.

Yoav folded the tables and chairs. Ruth convened the help
around the kitchen island and was counting out their cash.

David yelled over to Yoav, "Just leave it all by the foyer
closet." Tammy rose and David said, "Hold up, Tam."

He opened his wallet, which had one bill left inside. "Where you off to?"

Tammy went to take the bill but David lured it back until she said, "A thing."

"Another party?"

"I said a thing."

David yelled, "Yoav, just leave them, come here. Your cousin's taking you out to a party."

"Dad."

"Wherever it is, whatever it is, take him. Cab it."

"You're talking about him like he's not even here, Dad."

"So are you, Tam."

She hailed them a cab on the corner of Fifth and told the driver an address, unzipped her backpack and took out the bottle she'd swiped, swigged and passed. The driver rancored away in Arabic, to himself or just a specter.

There, alongside her, Yoav put together her face. It'd been too strong straight on. Now he could sit back and amass a profile. Tammy had a strong crooked nose, a broken arrow nose. And a rampant mane of unwashed brown with glimmers of what could've been blond or gray. She had dry skin on her chin and, when she leaned in, she whispered in garlic, salt, and scotch:

"Do you understand what he's saying?"

"Who?"

"The driver."

"He tells—he told his wife he must go to piss."

After crossing a bridge, they looped around for a complex of new sleek condos wavering over the water. The elevator was undersize and overly bright. They were going to the highest floor, PH. "Who is Penthouse?" Yoav said, but Tammy, who had her compact out and was blotting herself, was unimpressed and said, "Some donor."

The elevator snapped open to a vestibule jumbled with masks and shields and shields like masks, spears and umbrellas and bags. Turning the corner was like turning a volume knob, the ardent chanting becoming urgent and louder. Everything was white, every surface from the countertops and chopping-blocks to the oven. It was the people who provided the colors, their skintones and clothes did, their cloaks and robes, which Yoav wasn't able to parse whether they were the pinnacle of fashion or just suggestions for the curtains. The cityward wall was a window. There were pointy hats. There was a person in a checkered kafiya.

Tammy weaved around basketry that might've been for sit-ting on, around a bioethanol fireplace below a contiguity of monitors cycling a slideshow of children. They were writing with chalk on slats at a school. They were eating some type of flatbread next to a well. Doing gymnastics. Trampolining. Weav-ing something on looms. Tammy was checking rooms, slipped into a room, dropped her backpack and coat and rushed behind another door she spun to shut just as Yoav was coming in.

"Bathroom, hello? I'm going to the bathroom?"

Yoav startled, stepped back in apology. There, facing each other at the threshold, for a moment it was like they were danc-ing.

Later, when the lights went low, he'd get drunk enough to dance purposefully.

Tammy introduced him to her boss, a pallid woman who said she wasn't her boss: "No one works for me, every one of us works for the children."

"That's the issue with nonprofits," Tammy said, "the more money you're spending on internals, the less you have to spend on your mission."

A dashiki, a kimono, and a bundle of banker guys in banker suits mustered agreement and made an exit. The music was up and drumming.

Yoav had another shot of rum and then the shot he'd brought for Tammy.

The boss redraped herself in some burry wool serape that belonged between a saddle and donkey and swung herself into another conversation.

A girl brisked over. "Been fundraising?"

Tammy said, "Our asses off."

The girl said, "Boss'll be asking you to call her a car."

"Ten minutes she'll ask me."

"There's grinding going on. Ten seconds."

Tammy introduced the girl to Yoav as her friend, who also worked with her and was her roommate.

The girl smirked and told Yoav she was Tammy's friend, who also worked for her and was her tenant.

Tammy said, "Meet Cousin Yoav."

The girl said, "Five four three two one."

Their boss, from over by the window, yelled, "Tammy."

The explosion the girl made in her mouth became a croaky laugh. Tammy handed Yoav her champagne and he put his lips to her lipstick prints and drained.

"I said—you're Israeli?"

Yoav took the girl by the waist and swayed her. "The cousin of Tammy. One second removed."

The girl repositioned the chopsticks in her dreads. "So what happened? With Israel? You just couldn't cut it? Couldn't live there anymore?"

"I just try to make travel and do new things. New experience."

"I don't blame you."

"For what?"

"For whatever you did in the army."

Yoav stepped on his own sneaker. "And you? What you do?"

"I send emails. I update social media."

"About?"

"Genocides, environmental catastrophes, polio outbreaks at refugee camps in Palestine."

"That important."

"Vaccinations, reproductive rights, child conscription. I make lists of people who have money and invite them to this."

"Money for the children?"

"We help women too, but people care about children."

"Not the men?"

"If you're lucky enough not to be one of the 4.9% of all infants who die every year, then I'd say you have a roughly 50/50 chance of growing up to be a man."

"Then after they growing up you not help them?"

"Then they're on their own."

He was behind her, bumping up against her, up a spiral stairway to the roof, emerging onto a terrace sheathed in glass, with an awning he was sure was retractable.

To the north and south were towers, out in front was Manhattan, and all around were the airplanes for stars. But it wasn't enough. He wouldn't be satisfied until there was nothing above him. He boosted himself atop a cherryslat bench but could barely touch the awning or keep balanced.

"What are you doing?"

"I want to find the," he couldn't find how to say it, jumped down. "The thing for the roof," he said.

"What thing?"

"I want the," and he made a cranking motion with his hand and then blushed from its unmeant obscenity.

She'd already had the joint rolled and now licked it. "Just chill." She lit the fussed tip, sucked, and gave it to Yoav— "Tammy wouldn't approve," she said.

"She not like?"

"She does like, she just wouldn't approve."

Two tugboats hooted out on the water.

She took the joint back from Yoav and kissed him. Just a brief kiss, a meeting of teeth, and a retreat from his tongue.

"What's my name?"

She pushed him down onto a swiveling rocker and its bamboo crackled under his weight like flames. She steadied the rocker, angled it toward her and stood over him.

"Tell me one thing about me. One thing."

She undid his suitjacket and stroked his chest through the shirt and then she was undoing the shirt. He tried to help her but she swatted his hands, popped a button.

"Your name is Yoav. Y, O, A, V. And me, I'm a bicycle activist. A feminist who bakes. I'm also your cousin's intern. She's my landlord."

She took another toke and handed the joint off, sank down to her knees and put her face to his stomach, kissing him again at least there, kissing his muscles there, tonguing their each packaged definition.

"Here's what we have in common," she said. "I like to talk and you don't."

"Also," he said, "we both from Africa."

She laughed and hacked and undid his clasp, unzipped him and then, gripping his ridiculous suitpants by the ridiculous pleats, she pulled them folded around his scant socks and sneakers. She left his boxers on.

All Yoav was thinking was how Natan had been wrong about the order: it didn't always go, or didn't always have to go, kiss kiss, tits, dagdagan

He was hard.

All he was thinking was how Eli and Sami had been wrong about how American women liked to be forced: some liked to be the forcers.

He was missiles hard.

For now, though, she was just enjoying teasing him: nosing among his abs and biting, digging her nails along his ribs, burying her bitten nails between his ribs and then scraping up toward his nipples. She scraped just below his throat and poked his scar. That brownness. That raised puffy blackbrownness like a burn.

The Zelda, the APC, the vehicle was being shot up. They'd driven into a trap, on the way to reinforce the paratroopers, along that hoveled road between Jabalia and Shujaiyeh. This was their 12th day of combat. Grenades were skizzing in, the Zelda was treads on fire. Uri hauled him out through the hatch, because he wasn't getting out on his own. Shelter was a doorway and then Uri was ramming the door down and hauling him inside, which might've detonated an IED, or else they'd been grenaded. The jamb. A piece of the jamb—a piece from where its mezuzah would've been, had any dwelling in Gaza been a Jewish dwelling—mixed in with some shrapnel—had passed above his vest and lodged inside him.

In Yoav.

She pressed where it'd lodged, twisted the bump left by its removal like it was an ignition, squeezed it like she was piqued and wouldn't stop until she'd gotten a reaction. But he wasn't the one to be seeking that from.

Not Yoav sprawled in a castoff suit, his feet sliding along the tile, knees locked, head hung in smoke.

She rose up from the hollow of his legs to snatch the joint back. "You must be embarrassed."

She took a last toke and then spit in his navel, a dense taunting strand, and, as if with a sigh, put the joint out in the puddle.

"What happen?" Yoav said.

"I'm just making it worse."

She was standing again, embarrassed herself, because though she was still attracted to him, she'd just realized that what she was attracted to was his monstrousness.

Yoav, wrists smearing the ashy saliva, crept a hand into his boxers to tug his untouched cock. "Why you go? For condom?"

But she was already heeling beyond the giant potted ferns. "Sure, army boy, that's what I'm doing. I'm just going to get us a condom."

Yoav sat and dripped. The glass that immured was vast and streakless and admitted the city, some of it shimmering and some with a cauterizing clarity, as if to assert that there was no such thing as darkness, only distance. Darkness was just distance from light. He tossed the joint to a planter and brought his pants up.

Standing made him dizzy and he reached for support, but all there was to grasp was flat and slippery. He could only palm the panes, imprint them, he could only lean his head against them and cloud them with his breath.

Some of the towers were clad in glass and some just had glass for windows. All of them mirrored and were mirrored by their neighbors, just like the river and sky worked on each other by day, insatiably reflecting.

It was hard to fathom that there could be more, that more could fit—on the ground, in the air in his eye.

This tower Yoav was terraced on wasn't the tallest along the river, but it was the closest to the river, or the closest not still under construction—it was newly completed, which meant it was just a matter of months or even weeks before a newer tower went up between here and the Manhattan skyline, which ascended to the heavens like an emergency stairs to be used in case of fire.

Not out amid the night but directly down, below him, was the deep dirt pit for the newest, with a ladderlike structure already growing inside it.

Any day now its foundations would breach streetlevel and then, engirdered, climb higher, into a massive steel frame sustained by walls of glass.

He'd stand here until the drums went slack or the tower had risen to block his view.

✷

Uri's eldest and youngest sisters had been making some inquiries and one day between the holidays on the pretext of going to the GlobusMax and letting him decide between whichever was the current iteration of *Transformers* or *X-Men*, they borrowed the middle sister's boyfriend's car and the middle sister's boyfriend himself, Ben Sassoon, a 30 year old man boyfriend who was so consummately an accountant that he'd been an accountant in the army, and had him drive them all cramped out to a brittle stucco block, the groundfloor a shabby clothingstore selling shapeless floralprinted clothes for old women hung on mannequins with the bodies of young women that lacked heads and arms and legs, which were scattered to the floor of the display amid fallen flypaper and gluetraps.

This was the bargain they'd struck: if Uri just cooperated, just this once cooperated, his sisters would get him some hash. And then they'd come back in an hour, or in 45 minutes that were billed like an hour and get high with him, higher than the sun and then they'd all go to the GlobusMax, where it was dank and snacky.

Trembling—whether with anger or trepidation, it didn't matter, the trembling's the thing—Uri resisted, until his sisters said they'd be charged if he canceled, they'd be charged if he skipped and so, stuffing their scrimped cash into a pocket, he got out of the car and dawdled like an inmate in the courtyard, where the building kept its trash. And then the decision was which staircase. The hallways were all dingy white and the doors they led to were all the same and labeled something Ashkenaz: something like Mirsky and Hoffmann, the type of names that made him claustrophobic, Yudkevitz. Dentists, osteopaths. Accountants, of course.

And then the Psycholog, a professional with hips.

She wanted to know about his family—what they'd told him about this visit and how they'd told him and how that made him feel.

He said nothing, or not much. Which, she said, was a hallmark of adjustment troubles—transitions to civilian life were rarely smooth.

But Uri returned the next Sunday and gradually, he opened: he mentioned Batya, his father and the roofing job, his mother and the Prison Service job, the Baba Batra.

The Psycholog wanted to know what that renowned rabbi, so beloved of orphans and recovering addicts, had told him, so Uri told her.

"And you agree with him," the Psycholog said, "that the fight never ends?"

"It does end," Uri said, "but only with death."

"Did he say that?"

"I did."

"Do you think about death?"

"Whatever I say, you'll think I'm threatening suicide."

"Are you?"

"And anyway who knows what happens after we die? Not me or you. Not even the religious have a concept. We Jews—do you know this, that we Jews have the only major world religion that tells its people what to eat and when and where to pray and even how to fuck, but nothing at all about what it'll be like after God rolls the credits?"

"Didn't your rabbi tell you that Judaism believes in the coming of the messiah?"

"And we'll all be resurrected—that's what you believe? But what happens between, in all that time between death and resurrection? Do we get to keep our phones? Will there be service—a signal?"

"And what about Jews who don't have phones—what will they do?"

"What Jews don't have phones? Anyway, I'm not here to debate religion with you."

The Psycholog smiled gnarly incisors. "You're not here to debate religion, OK—so tell me what you're here for."

He was about to say: for your thighs. Instead he said, "For my sisters and because the rabbi didn't cure me."

The Psycholog adjusted her skirt. "That's it?"

"And the dreaming."

The Psycholog's face took on that late in the session distance like she was scouting over his head to the land beyond the clock. "You can never choose your dreams or your family, but you can choose how you react to them."

"Fine, sure."

"And yet you don't react, at least you don't so that anyone notices, having been conditioned to internalize all the frustration and aggression. You punish yourself for letting yourself be punished by others."

"OK."

"Tell me, then, how can you expect to benefit from this consultation, or even from a session of blessings from a criminal rabbi, if you've been pressured to go—or not just pressured but nearly physically compelled? No one before has ever given you the choice of what to do, but now it's time to give yourself that choice and you're flailing and I wonder why—I wonder how that feels to you?"

"Cool."

"Whose father—yours? What about him?"

"I said cool."

"No—no—don't censor yourself. You were about to say something about your father."

"Whatever."

But then analysis can only be described in the language in which it's conducted, because psychology is language, and *sababu* is "cool" and *ubu* is "father."

Uri unfolded his arms from his chest and picked at the laminate curled loose from the tissuebox table.

The Psycholog sighed and said, "Let's propose for a moment that I'm mistaken and you said *cool*—then what? Aren't you just capitulating? Being obedient? Compliant? Because the bonds of family were never severed but merely transferred to the army, postponing maturation so that even now you don't know your own emotions? You don't know if you're capable of living autonomously? So let's propose instead, just as an experiment, that regardless of what you meant or intended to mean you unequivocally said *father*—how to treat that? Wouldn't it be logical that in a house like yours, so full with women—your manipulative sisters who sent you to me and your mother who sent you to that fraud kabbalist who extends refuge to child molesters and condones domestic abuse—wouldn't it be logical that in a house like that, your father would be your most natural ally, your most natural model? But then maybe he's weak too? Maybe he never showed you how to stand up and take back what's yours?"

Aba, sababa, the Baba Batra: Uri stood, but everything he might've said curdled in his mouth unpronounceable.

He put a tissue to his face and spit.

Their time was up, and that was their final time: this second session. Uri never went to the office again, he just called once and left a voicemail to say that he'd found someone closer, though he also said that this someone was cheaper too and then, irked by his own remark, closed by thanking the Psycholog gratuitously as if politeness would preclude her from phoning his sisters to check up.

He felt low—this was the worst of him. To be hiding out like this, to be slinking out of the house keeping secrets from his secrets. Sitting in a field. Like a wanking mystic. Lying on a blanket in a field like he used to do with Batya. Except now without Batya, who he was betting would follow the example of Michal Tash and Liat Stalbet, one who just got engaged to her middleaged boss at Bezeq, the other who went out to the Bay Area of California and got herself knocked up, not just by a goy but by a Turk. All according to Uri's sisters. A bitch, a cunt, pretentious. Batya and her clique, not Uri's sisters—who were generous and kind, willing to sacrifice anything for control of him.

They kept slipping him their money and because Uri couldn't stop them, he could only justify himself, he kept up the ruse: having never mentioned that he'd quit the Psycholog, he still honored his appointments.

He left the house with Yarden, the youngest, and waited for her to take her sherut and only then took his and rode it until his returning would seem plausible or later—he'd stay out at the movies or just outside in the weather, when it wasn't too hot, when the duplicity overpowered. It appalled him, to be pocketing his sisters' money—maybe not Yarden's contribution, because it came from his parents anyway, from the tuition allotment they still gave her, and maybe not Orly's, the middle sister's, either, because it'd been carnally embezzled from Ben Sassoon, the accountant, whom her parents were nagging her to marry—rather it was Amit's, the eldest's, whose dull coins clinked against the heart, as they'd been made straightening frizzy curls for weddings, depilating, buffing, dyeing brides.

Uri had become a man who lived off women, off family-women, and was petrified of his father.

Why did he stop attending these Psycholog sessions? Why didn't he tell his sisters he'd stopped? Why couldn't he? And why was it that he felt the need to mention to his father—who hadn't asked anything about how Uri had been spending his time—that he, Uri, had gone to work for a Kurdish mechanic at a Paz station near Beit Kama?

These are all questions he might want to ask should his consultations ever resume.

His one consolation was that his tradecraft was consistent—it was consistently excellent. He never missed the chance to miss a session even on days when nobody was home to notice whether he left when he was supposed to.

It wasn't that he was concerned about Mrs. Shavit, the widow nextdoor, who could be as nosy at the window as she was regular in naps. Neither was he concerned about his sisters, whose curiosity about their therapeutic investment could be satisfied by his usual mutterings or, lately, by an unusually imperious appeal to the policy of doctor/patient confidentiality he'd gleaned from a book he'd shoplifted from the mall's Steimatzky.

Instead, he just worried about himself—about maintaining discipline. About not letting down Mr. Gil and Mr. Yitz, the sherut drivers who split the Netivot route and expected him weekly—roundtrip cost 20 shekels.

The sherut was a 1996 Mercedes Benz Sprinter City and on any given day there'd be, Uri would make report to himself, about six or seven other passengers: always the earbuds and eyedrops girl and then occasionally this other adolescent Haredi girl who waited for the newest paved sections of road to slather on her unguents and extirpate her pimples.

Once the sherut had broken down, one Sunday, and Mr. Gil had requested help, because Mr. Yitz had told him Uri was a mechanic. Uri didn't remember having told Mr. Yitz that, but found himself clamping down on a deltoid and forced to clarify: he was still just an apprentice mechanic.

Everything in the desert became like the desert—everything dusted a caffeine brown spread by tiretread into blackness until all the signs and radomes and satellite dishes and even the roads and their barriers appeared indigenous. And in Beersheva and Kiryat Gat all the bars had seemed like real bars, but they were shit. And in Netivot the poolhall had seemed like it had a real bar too, but it was shit, and the hash there was too cheap to be hash but still, for him, too expensive and made his head feel as if it were full up with clearcolored gummiworms. But this route's only other options were Sderot, which wasn't really a city, and the moshavim and kibbutzim, which weren't really anything or even trying.

Everything in this country was trying to pass for what it wasn't. Everything was camouflaged in this desert of a country.

The sherut was stifling—the AC was busted and Uri had substances in his blood. Also he'd be coming back too early. And there were boulders. He'd forgotten how happy boulders made him. How happy he'd be if he got off, clambered up them, caressed them, and then thumbed it the rest of the way. On the 25, the highway.

He leaned toward the driver's seat and tapped Mr. Yitz and requested a stop and Mr. Yitz nodded into the rearview mirror, "Achi, gever, relax, you paid me to take you to Nika," so Uri yelled, "I'm asking you to stop," and Mr. Yitz said, "And I'm asking you to stay seated, you're freaking out the passengers," but the only other passenger was this Bedouin who'd been scrolling women on his phone and who now stayed motionless and averted, doing a convincing imitation of an unattended bag.

Uri kept yelling until Mr. Yitz said, "Nu, b'seder, be crazy," though still he drove on but slower, slumping the sherut toward the shoulder's sand, as if he found the prospect of dropping a passenger alone in the flattened wastes distasteful, or not just that, but inevitable and distasteful, and the way he strained his head over the wheel and twitched between the windows communicated his disappointment if not with Uri or himself, then with their nation, which wasn't providing even the slightest hint of a civilization deserving of his brakes: just a stretch of fencing and the stalks of sprinklerheads sprouted around a single transplant cedar.

Uri jumped out at some industrial park and the sherut limped away like a fox lamed in a fight and stunned by daylight.

This was a smidge after the Ha'Nasi junction and the time according to the sun was 16:00 something.

Which meant that Binyamin would just be rousting a stewardess out of his bed before scootering to Port Metro Vancouver. Avi would be sipping a coffee, or sitting to squeeze out a coffee shit, or just stuck in fucking traffic again because he had to bring this buxom snubnosed HVAC salesrep home on his way to the appliance showroom at the Plaza Carso Polanco. Yaniv, he'd be rolling up his sleepingbag like a Viennese pastry, the kind whorled with chocolate or currant jam. As for Moti and Dani, they'd be on a train to Buchenwald or Dachau, but for a tour—which meant they'd be drunk too or just hungover already.

And Yoav—he was running the family business. He'd inherited it. He was halfway to being a millionaire by now. But only halfway—and he needed Uri, according to Uri, to carry him like a pack up to the peak of the cliff and show him how to spend what was below them.

That same blue Kia that'd passed him once already was approaching again in the opposite direction. Must've been turned around. Didn't want to go to the Bedouin town. What a sad notion, a Bedouin town. Uri felt it in his spine, that sensation of being an obstruction. He searched the landscape for weapons, that's how he was trained, to search around whatever surroundings for anything to weaponize. In the poolhall, he might've gone for a poolcue and swung it. In the bars there'd been steins to smash and the cash register would've been hard enough to crack any jaws he bashed against it. But here, nothing like that was available here. There was just a stunted tamarisk to uproot and wield. A grass clod to fling in the face. Sand to kick in desperation. The desert was its own defense. It would just let the car keep driving and driving for dunams, offering up nothing of its own to hit—just him.

The Kia, in that kabbalist blue, the blue that wards off evil, veered onto the shoulder, straight at him. Uri stepped toward the guardrail and the Kia swerved sidelong, skidded long, throwing up a nimbus of dust that concealed both leftside doors opening and the guys who leapt out.

Uri came to in the trunk.

Though later he'd maintain that he'd never tapped out or if he had then it hadn't been from being tackled but from the trunk lid banging his scalp.

He'd known immediately what'd happened and he'd even claim that he'd known by the traffic alone—by the ambient honking and neon in through the seams—that he was being driven through Tel Aviv.

He was already laughing about it by evening but had too much dignity to ask how many times Eitan and Oded had tailed him.

As for calling his family, he'd call his family himself.

He slept with his squadmates on mats on the floor of some studio that was otherwise furnitureless because it was a krav maga studio and though they weren't supposed to be living there the owner was benevolent or just a moron.

The owner of Adam Greenberg Judo, Aikido, & Krav Maga was Adam Greenberg—Kivsa Brigade, Akavish Battalion, Tziraah Company, but class of 2008: too old for First Gaza, too young for Second Lebanon.

Eitan taught at the studio four sessions a day and unloaded boxes at night, produce for the shuk Ha'Carmel and the market on Levinsky, dairy for a dozen or so AM:PMs. Oded taught two night sessions and spent the day doing data entry for Keter Plastic. Between jobs they made plans to launch their own studio. Which entailed a physical studio with equipment and a website. But before that, before they could even reckon a budget, they had to hone their method. They'd been developing their own martial art but had no guiding ideology, though by the time they explained this to Uri they'd become so stymied by the struggle to define one that they were ready to accept that a martial art shouldn't have a guiding ideology—because all an ideology did was limit options—violence was what happened after ideology failed.

Uri, meanwhile, found the address of the offices of Appikoros, Inc. He asked for Batya Neder and was told she'd moved to Brussels. Which he was told was in Belgium, which he resented. He asked for her manager or the man who'd managed to lay her and the receptionist summoned a man who Uri knew wasn't him, he knew was a guard, who was old and fat and had the posture of someone who'd sat protractedly in tanks. Uri punched him in the face and walked back to the studio. The walk took all night because of the bars and in the morning he was vomiting green gin all over the grating. Greenberg tossed everyone out. Eitan threatened to quit. Oded talked to Greenberg, who in a crisis of sniveling admitted that the decision wasn't his, the studio wasn't even his, it was his mother's, at least it was her name on the lease. Eitan and Oded went to talk to the mother, who let them stay but charged them rent, though she refused to take in Uri too and gave him just a week to make alternate arrangements. As a Slav, she had no tolerance for darker skin and for anyone who had no tolerance for alcohol. Uri still had about 1,200 shekels of sisterly Psycholog money. Eitan contacted their squadmates, Oded set up a crowdfunding account. Another 3,634 shekels would turn their problem into Yoav's problem. What hadn't quite been a kidnapping demanded what wasn't quite a ransom: if the squad didn't pay up, Uri would have to go home.

✺

LET MY PEOPLE STAY

—sign on a house facing foreclosure,
Wakefield, Bronx, NY, Christmas 2012

AVERY LUTER, IMAMU NABI

(Another Occupation)

WINTER knocks once, and then knocks the door down, unrolls its white prayer rug over everything. Winter, that once a year prayer. You've got to be ready for it—start weeks early, start months early—unless you try to escape by getting yourself bussed down to Florida, in which case, best of luck. But if you intend to stay, to dig in and fight it, you're going to have to be prepared, with sufficient guts and wood to burn: the branches before the fenceposts, the fenceposts before the furniture. Come the solstice, which is life's shortest day, you're going to want to make your fire: your first fire, it won't be your last. Get a bucket of snow, warm it up into water, wash and dry yourself thoroughly, get your clothes together into layers from tightest to loosest, pronouncing the Shahada throughout to set your mind—to show all that whiteness outside the true meaning of purity: there is no god but Allah and Muhammad is His messenger . . .

If ever you needed evidence, if ever you needed definitive proof that white is evil and black is natural and good, just remember outerspace, and how outerspace is black, the universe is black, and black is peace because it's the absence of color.

And then recall that winter is white and hopelessly cold and so many brothers are dying . . .

His name was Imamu Nabi, and this was what he believed.

Imamu Nabi wasn't his legal name but fuck legal.

He was a man of many beliefs and of frustrations that'd hardened into hatreds. He hated the US Department of Veterans Affairs for its incompetence at delivering his essential services and the US Postal Service for its competence at delivering his inessential mail. His bills and postdues. His collection agency and debt consolidation correspondence. He hated the Port Authority of New York & New Jersey and how the midget culero from the Malopolskie Bakery sometimes tied up live rats into the bags of stale bread he tossed to the curb. He hated the Lincoln Savings Bank, later acquired by Anchor Bancorp, which in a merger became Dime Bancorp, later acquired by Washington Mutual, which in its failure amid the general failure that was the Great Recession of Anno Hegirae 1428–1430 was seized, placed in receivership, and reassetized to JPMorgan Chase, which was the entity that now held the note on his home. And so it wasn't his anymore, it wasn't a home anymore. It was theirs, just a house.

And he especially hated how when the snow got sooty, when it got all tinted with the car pollutions, the whitefolks said and even the blackfolks said, that snow be dirty, yo. Because the snow wasn't dirty. The folks be wrong, yo, and that might've been the only thing all the folks have ever had in common, their wrongness. Because that midday exhaust coloration, the CO_2 emissions melanization of the snow, was just the city trying to melt the day away for the children to get to school.

He was born Avery Luter in spring in Texarkana, the Arkansas side. His father, who'd served as a janitor in the fight against Hitler, had returned, fathered him and, wrongplaced, wrong-timed, was arrested for riding in the same car as the gate attendant and the stolen gate strongbox of a traveling circus rodeo. He was convicted of one count of armed robbery, two counts of assault, and sent to pick cotton on a prison farm in Texas. Avery's mother took her son, aged two months, to Harlem to live with her uncle and aunt, who'd procured her a position as typist in the office of a haircare products manufacturer (relaxants, straighteners, wave tonics), which gave bonuses to employees whose children made high grades. Avery made high grades and avoided trouble. His subjects were Citizenship, Geometry, Biology, and Choo Choo Coleman of the New York Metropolitans. He once had his hand shook by Mayor Wagner.

He was an indoor child of three strict Christian parents (none of whom mentioned the parent jailed), the family was an indoor family.

A year after he turned 18, he rolled a 4 in the Vietnam draft, and you did what your country told you, even if your country told you Chu Lai. Americal Division, Alpha Company, 1st of the 96th. He was a machinegunner, shot foliage, lizards, gooks. For trying to shoot him, for making the rain, making the heat, taking his zzz's away. Everything the fault of the gook. Gun fails to chamber or cock, fucking gooks. Too rainy, so the chopper can't land, not enough heat tabs so you're just chowing on raw rabbit, blame the gooks. His CO was a gook, all America was. America that sent him from the back of the bus to the front lines, to die. America its own enemy, which needed the brothers to beat the gooks, but also wanted the gooks to get rid of the brothers so America didn't have to.

Boots and feet the same leather, scragged up, skin peeling back to gook yellow, gook white. Punji wounds, scorching dragonchasing dragonlady fevers. For which he sought the succor of Christ, Who madeth his enemies fall in green paddies and shepherded him atop Hill 411—where his platoon was pinned, where the howitzers devoured half his platoon, leaving the other half for the poppy and poon. His nicknames were Bible, Brillo Head, Iggernay, and Tarbaby, his rank upon discharge was Specialist 4.

Back Stateside he alternated stints as a busboy and later a waiter with periods of unemployment and boozing. Then he'd go broke, his mother wouldn't let him borrow, and he'd get that conscience again, get clean. He enrolled in but never completed the Borough of Manhattan Community College. He got a Japanese classmate pregnant, paid for the girl's abortion, read books.

Two friends died, one definitely a suicide: from a deuce or trey of adulterated Schmeck, Manthrax speedballed. Another got hit by an ambulance and even that had to do with Vietnam. Some friends who survived became Panthers, others were cats always changing their spots. Getting into Rasta, into Black Hebraism, Nation of Islam. Blacks were created before the sun and stars, their dark forms dug out from the void. The moon used to be part of the earth until the imams invented dynamite and blew it skyward. Avery didn't embrace or even judge the tenets, he just liked their refusals, their rage. He himself would frequently slag on the Hymies—the Jewdog usurers, the Zionist pawnbrokers, the overcharging underpaying predatory loaning don't patch no leaky ceiling kikes—but then he got along and once even got a reuben sandwich with his BMCC American History instructor, Professor Jacob C. Friedman, and liked his boss, Yossi, at Loco Joe BBQ, just fine.

He never told them, never even told his mother, he converted—took the Shahada, and another name too: Imamu Nabi.

Officially, though, he was still Avery Luter. He never bothered with the paperwork, never had the patience or trust for it.

In 1978 he landed a job with the Port Authority as a toll collector.

It was a decent job or was thought to be because it was difficult to get, you had to be connected. Imamu's connection was his mother's man, who was a PA payroll supervisor.

The expectation of gratitude embittered Imamu, as did his assignment to the tunnels, never the bridges: he thought he was being denied fresh air because of his race. Hours and hours standing hurt in his stockingfeet making change, the Holland nastier than the Lincoln. Still, he had to admit the job improved things: he now owned a waterbed, a Marantz stereo, and an Adire tiedye that partitioned the kitchen from the rest of his pad, corner of 185th & How Do You Like Them Apples Boulevard.

He also, a line at a time, was able to read in the booth, books from the library that complicated his certainties and realigned his faith. White and black was just a battle, he realized, even Vietnam had been just a battle, in the Armageddon war between chattel capitalism and the precariat. Money was the god of the mosques, where the honorable ministers tapdanced for tithes like Carolina Baptists who'd just moved north and clipped on bowties. None of them had done the hajj or even marched on Washington. He tried other mosques in abutting hoods but they all just skewed too beardy. With real Arabs from real Arabia. Clannish, zealous, katam and henna. He was brought back to the church tragically and so only temporarily in 1996, when his mother stroked out and died and, given her minimal savings and that her man, who was never her husband, was now living with dementia with his own children in Maryland, the funeral expenses were his. He buried her and, having inherited her house, took out a second mortgage.

The house was massive and stately but in Ornan Fields— way out in the outerboroughs, threshed and harrowed. Imamu was going to sell and then he wasn't. No one was buying. Because of the mortgages and projects. The stabbings, shootings, arsons. He taught himself plumbing and electric, he learned how to install a stove.

In 2001 he was finally reassigned to the George Washington Bridge and immediately robbed—not injured, just robbed. He found himself under suspicion to the point that he suspected himself: he'd been begging for the transfer and then, the moment the transfer was granted, this white Camaro comes cruising in low and erratic and this high sureño punk put a gun to his head, he didn't know what type of gun but he knew sureño and white Camaro. The faces the PA detectives kept showing him were black. He was having headaches and vein issues. He kept switching between the compression socks and the diabetic socks until he wore them both and had become allergic to the gloves that kept the filth of money from his hands. The PA detectives were curious about his myriad names and his being a Muslim. His booth's prayer calendar got defaced and his radio taken. He filed a complaint against the swingshift and found himself reassigned again to the Outerbridge Crossing—the furthest assignment he could get.

His days were spent commuting and in Midtown bouts of trying to identify faces that couldn't exist and cars and guns he was hallucinating: a guy as black as him with his old corroded bolt M60 behind the wheel of a 2888 Chevy Sureño.

His hood: the Blooded and Cripped, having divided the turf, rode the DMZ between the Garveys and Wentworth Arthur Matthew. The Baby A's had the front of the Hattusa Houses, the EEU crew had the back, and in the middle was a territorial dispute, both sides of which were being governed from Rikers.

The Brimless Boys slung their zips below the scaffold of the Ammon Air Rights Rehab, across from PS 613, and even across from the masjid, between which was the lone bodega equipped to sell him, if he had the cash to buy, his minty Cope dips, and all the three ingredients of Robitussin Wine, the third ingredient being the pineapple Jolly Ranchers. The pills the doctor prescribed for his vein pain were stronger than any opiate he remembered—so strong they got him fired after he nodded on the job.

He was already six months behind on his monthlies, envelopes lay scattered on the porch. Which gave the impression that his house was abandoned, his house was unmanned. Kids would be fixing to burgle. Kids just trying to find a place to get crunked, a place to strip of copper.

He sat in noddy vigil over his mother's bequest. His mother's furniture. Armoires, breakfronts, credenzas, stuff that wasn't made anymore. Legs like of beasts, arms swathed in lace.

If he left, because he had to leave, he just went to the Key

Food and the library, not the one by the projects that didn't have any computers or the one by the autobodies with just a row of so slow they might as well have been unplugged computers, but the J to the Sixth Avenue Line to the Main Manhattan, that library temple of studiers so mindfully wise they didn't always keep track of their backpacks, serious soap and paper replenishment action in the bathrooms, shelves of probate property records, and a whole entire room of genealogy like a grove of familytrees.

Default: failure to fulfill an obligation—automatic reversion to a predetermined option. *Foreclose*: to deprive—to shut out, exclude, bar—to prevent—to establish an exclusive claim to— to close, settle, answer beforehand.

A brother from the masjid was a lawyer, but an immigration lawyer from Pakistan, who gave him a number to call and Imamu called and the party rang him back but gave no advice, just made an offer on the property, plug nickels on the dollar.

The Pakistani lawyer followed up but by then he was already buying himself free of pain on the street, because his COBRA insurance had lapsed, and Verizon had terminated his phoneservice.

After he flunked a drugtest his union rep was through with him. No appeal.

He'd told the Baby A's he wanted more of the same—he'd wanted more oxy. But they'd offered rocks, a zip for free. He repeated himself like a child to a child. Other crews offered h. He repeated himself into mumbling, just wandering the leafblown pedways mumbling, the only child who wasn't armed.

He left the house once a day, stayed out all day to avoid being served, and returned by night to kick the envelopes from off the porch. He returned, once, to find the door padlocked and papered with petition.

Notice of Eviction—winter was hereby proclaimed.

Imamu felt the inadequacy of having missed something— like how you feel if you're religious and missed some prayer. The time for its pronouncement just crept up on you and now all you can do is await the retribution.

Christmas. Red and green, the colors of traffic, became the colors of the season. Snow fell in dustings, a blanket. He needed a blanket. His shoes were crap. He went out to shop, to spend what he had left: his senses.

Outside the Key Food was a market of Christmas trees and each day until the sixth business day he dragged trees home with him—dragging them after him like tightly furled umbrellas through a basement window he'd shattered. The culeros paid to guard the artificial forests would be in their folding-chairs asleep.

He'd go for the smaller trees, which dried quicker.

The hearth he'd renovated himself. He'd put in the flue, he'd once scooped a dead possum out of the chimney.

He'd also stolen a hatchet out from under the noses of the sleeping culeros and wore it in his waistband like an Indian. He was sure he had that heritage in him or recalled his mother saying he did or else just thought he recalled her saying that and that's what saddened him the most about not being able to talk to his mother anymore and never having known his father, that he wasn't able to do anything more than just wish himself a Comanche, Caddo, or Shango. Talk about garnishment, talk about repossession. Any tree just growing out on the curb unclaimed, its ownership reverted to whoever had the hatchet and the largest shiniest set of ornamental balls. The house was drowned in pine. He sat by the hearth and chopped the stolen pine and warmed himself by chopping and then spread out beside the grated flames atop a floor of needles.

Kwanzaa, which began the day after Christmas, ended on New Year's Day. The first night's theme was Umoja, meaning Unity: to strive for and maintain unity in the family, community, country, and race.

The last night was Imani, meaning faith.

✽

He was being told how to pick stuff up and move it. Not with the back, with the knees. He was being told how to move stuff and put it down. How to hold it. How to position it. Uri, put it down. In the direction of use, open side up. Detailed instructions on how to deal with a cup. A cup was not a mug was not a glass, which, however, might be made out of glass. A plate was a dish not as deep as a bowl. Escalera, carretilla, vámonos coño. It was like being a grunt again, taking orders from shechorim, kushim.

Your-ee, they said. Only the Mexicanim said it his way, Or-ee.

He wasn't very good at it, Uri: neither the moving, nor the language. He was too impatient to be good. Anything that was said to him had to be said through Yoav. Anything he said in response would have to be transmitted the same in reverse. But something would happen to the words en route. They'd depart someone's mouth in English or his own mouth in Hebrew only to arrive way off in the target language like a casualty, hemorrhaging significance and finally expiring amid the interference and crosstalk.

Yoav refused to put into Hebrew the crew's cursing at Uri and to put into English Uri's cursing at him—Yoav was the only one to take the blame in the original.

Yoav was the only one to understand what Uri was up to: he was trying to justify, he was trying to earn, the demotion he perceived.

Uri had always had seniority. He'd been the active one, the valiant one, fluent at everything physical, while Yoav had always been the fretting junior, inattentive, blanching. But here in the States all that had changed and Uri wasn't quite able to concede. All his commands were going unobeyed because untranslated, and all his efforts to correct Yoav, like he'd always corrected Yoav, felt like desperate vestiges of days with higher stakes.

Which just made him work harder, which just made things break.

Moving was requiring all his strength along with a strangely sparing delicacy and so it contained a contradiction. In that way, Uri thought, it was like handling a woman—it was like handling Batya, the only other task at which he'd failed.

They were moving an office: nondescript, gray. It was a high floor all of windows and Uri sat in a revolving chair he was supposed to be packing at a desk he was supposed to be packing too and together they were turning into a Lockheed C130 soaring in splendor through the grayness and he was a paratrooper about to be airdropped atop the enemy theater of Jersey City just below, and then Paul Gall was calling his name—and Uri leapt, but leapt up, and stood in humiliation at having had his fantasy observed, and then he took hold of the chair and rolled it into the hall, toward Yoav at the elevators.

He rolled it at Yoav, but the carpeting was so thick that the chair made it only part of the way, then tipped.

Uri went up to a Midtown middlefloor office divvied up by collapsible cubicles and he pushed them over, he pushed them one by one, until the floor was a pile of walls.

He assembled pyramids out of modular filingunits scuffed and dinged and had Yoav propel him atop a dolly into them, and his body rebounded off them, ricocheted between them, until they knocked him down.

Boxes—they'd come flat and Uri would fold them together, flap over flap, but then he'd forget to seal them, so the flaps wouldn't hold, the flaps would give way, and Tom Gall would reprimand Yoav and then Yoav would reprimand Uri, who'd revenge himself by binding the next box with nearly a complete roll of tape as if he were unrolling around it a cloying length of his own innards and then he'd sever the length with his teeth.

When he'd throw a box to Tinks, say, or to anyone else on the crew, he'd have to say something in English, something like "Head up" or "Heads," but when he'd throw to Yoav, it was Hebrew: squared off, heavy, packed.

"What're we eating tonight?" "Where can I get a jacket for winter?" "Where's that bar your girl cousin works at?" "Think she'll ever let me tap that pussy?"

"I'm making hamin." "Bloomingdale's or Macy's." "Not Manhattan." "No."

Once, in the atrium of a skyscraper, Uri took a great glass globe off a pillar and threw it to Yoav, and the instant it was out of his hands, he just forgot—it was like he'd thrown away all memory of what he was throwing and whom he was throwing it to and which language to speak and what words.

Yoav was looking away—he was expecting Uri to carry it to him, not expecting him to throw it. But the globe arced across the atrium like a dazzling transparent bomb, and the motion caught the corner of his eye, so Yoav turned and grasped for it, and the glass slipped through his outstretched hands and burst atop the marble floor like an alien word into noise and millions of baffling glyphic filaments.

Tom was yelling hoarse. Yoav, holding his head, said it was his fault. This time, Uri didn't correct him. Everything was his fault, because Uri hadn't changed.

Yoav took the broom and swept. Uri went to wrap the empty pillar.

He was acting like a homo now, Yoav, with all his cleaning and cooking and dressing in khakis and plaids that though they fit too tight he wore them when they went out and even when they stayed home to ice their arms and he'd put on movies in English that were so old they weren't set in color and if Uri clicked the TV to a better channel he'd escape upstairs with his computer. Yoav was reading a lot and had stopped, Uri was taken aback by this the most, eating meat. At least he wouldn't eat it more than once or twice or three times a week. He'd gotten new shell glasses and new round earring studs and the ears around them festered red because in the piercing they'd been infected and the infection was only now going down.

Lately, Uri had noticed that Yoav was going to bed or just into his bedroom unsociably early, claiming spasms and pangs and pretending to sleep, switching off the overhead bulb but switching on a flashlight—like they used to do in the army after curfew. The nights when all the squad would masturbate. Or when they'd pretend to masturbate, so as to be left alone with their phone solitaire and farts. Each barrack bunk creaking to its own affinity, soldiers just shadows within lambent wombs of blanket.

Uri would creep upstairs and crouch by the door and watch Yoav's flashlight beam glide past the draft and listen to the gargling he wasn't able to put into meaning, though he was sure the same lines were being repeated but hushed—it was either a script or a psalm.

Once, after the flashlight went off and the dark was unspoken, he'd prowled over from his child's bedroom nextdoor and popped the knob and stood hovering over his friend's slumbering face, smeared with fleecy creams. He took his friend's glasses off the nightstand and tried them on and found the lenses clear and without prescription. In his friend's money drawer, there wasn't much money, just hairgels and a deodorant but not antiperspirant stick that Uri sniffed and rubbed into his pits and replaced among the clipped receipts and MTA maps and Playbills and a black & white stack of promotional photographs of some guy—some spiked stubbled guy cupping his chin and smiling and then again not cupping his chin and not smiling and weirdly it was only in the photos that had glasses and earrings that Uri recognized Yoav and he tacked the glossies up all around the house, even in the fridge and freezer.

That was how they filled their days off. They went to a bar that Yoav said Tammy was working at, but she wasn't there and when it came time for them to pay the drinks weren't free or even cheaper. Anyway, Uri did most of the drinking. Then they went to another bar, where a girl greeted them by saying, "You'll get what you were promised, Ahmed, but first I want my uranium."

Yoav, who had to be Ahmed again, had to strain for his lines: "One thing you Americans," and then again, "One thing you Americans," and she said, "Will never understand," and he said, "One thing you Americans will never understand is that we live here."

"You call this living?" she said.

He said, "For you, Madam Secretary, Baghdad is just a part-time job."

She singed an orange peel and floated it to finish the tumbler she handed to Uri, "Sec. Re. Tar. Y. And it's parttime job, not parrhtimeyob. You need to articulate."

He said, "Parrhtimeyob."

She said to Uri, "Dumbest script I ever read in my life."

She took them to the party of another friend from their acting class who didn't appreciate Uri draining most of the handle of Overholt she'd been saving for the eggnog.

Nobody at the party had hash or even a clue how to get hash but that was compensated for by the pot, whose nugs resembled unripened cocoons and weren't to be smoked but vaped until Uri's brain flew out of his mouth all wet and winged and gooey and purpurogenous. He streaked around the deck trying to catch it. But it squeezed through his fists and inside and down the hall into a bedroom under the bed, squeaking. A blond elf followed and crawled down beside him under the bed and tried to catch it too but the roommate friend whose room this was came strutting in dramatizing her drowsiness and the blond elf wriggled away and pulled herself up, pulled Uri up and said, "Where did your brain fly to next?"

Uri burped.

So she tried again, "Where do you live?"

"New York."

"Brooklyn?"

"Queens?"

"Too bad, too far, your brain might be lost."

New Year's Eve, which is just another night for Israelis, they went to meet the blond elf at a Manhattan club and lined between roped poles in the cold only to be turned away by a neckless black doorguy who didn't have their names, which he didn't even have them try spelling for him, listed on his tablet. Uri wouldn't accept that and was getting offended by Yoav's inability or just unwillingness to explain his nonacceptance. He was drunk a little and high a little too. He had to get inside, he had to dance in the warmth, not just outside to get warm. He had to go to the bathroom. The doorguy was ignoring Uri to talk into his wrist. Uri picked the wireless bud from out of his ear, like he wanted to hear the plan for himself. He wanted to hear the voice of God. Instead, he just got a bouncer striding toward him, "Sir, excuse me, sir?" while tugging a baton out from under his trench. "Can you please just step to the side?" Uri aped the accent and stepped, but sprung and took the bouncer out at the knees. Down on the sidewalk, he snatched the baton away and swung it for a perimeter while inflicting a litany of Hebrew insult: "I put my dick on your list, I put my dick on your line, I put my dick on your club, I put my dick on you"—"to put your dick on something" meaning "to not give a fuck about something."

The doorguy was going for help but Yoav cut in behind and gripped his camelhair coat and flipped it over his head, leaving him hooded and lurching witless and dropping his tablet to crack and glow, alongside the bouncer flat on the sidewalk who'd stopped returning the Hebrew profanities and was now just laughing in gasps.

His name was Arik, he was from Rishon L'Tzion and it turned out that he'd served in the tank corps with Shlomo's— their squad's Shlomo's—brother. "The older brother?" "The younger." "Which unit?" "Saar, Seventh Division."

And that was that, with apologies to the doorguy.

The club was good because the pills Tinks had provided were good. Uri took a whole while Yoav, pretending to wholeness, bit his halved, which Uri noticed and he reached into Yoav's mouth and plucked the half out and swallowed that too. They paced the simulated combat conditions on a hunt for elfin blondes. Uri went to the bathroom. It was so hard in this city to know who was homo. Another hard thing was knowing how to dress. When he was done, Yoav wasn't where he'd left him. Uri's best dance moves were Running Robot, STrance, Na Nach, and Manic Absorption. Then Yoav was behind him doing spastic calisthenics and then Arik was too and then this other Israeli named Zeev, an artillerist from Arad who'd flown drones in the army and now worked the club's lighting and sound. They brought Uri and Yoav out to the fireescape for the fireworks and stood in rapture as the sky burned. After the club closed they went to a bar that stayed open for bartenders and DJs. Uri was wearing a shearling he'd thieved from off a banquette. They went to a diner and Yoav got a waitress to charge his phone. The way Uri was ordering they could never go home. Zeev had a Crown Vic the color of skim milk filled with cereal marshmallow clovers and rainbows and plastic dinosaur toys and Yoav and Uri sat on either side of the child's carseat and were driven out over the river as far as Zeev could go before being inconvenienced, Broadway Junction.

The sun was already peaking as they descended underground. To the blue circle A train, bearing down with its evil eye headlight. Yoav sat but Uri liked standing, touching nothing but himself. No stripperpoles, no monkeybars, no seats. He liked, when the train stopped, when it screeched and stopped abruptly, trying to maintain his balance. It was like trying to surf on the back of a vomiting blue dolphin. The walls of the tunnel felt like the walls of the train felt like his skin— everything, all together, was in motion.

Uri just let Yoav lead and was content to follow. That's what Uri was doing here, following. Letting Yoav feel important. With his little bitch language and his little bitch phone. They were the green wobbly dot on its map. The directions were telling them to turn and they turned, onto a wider street that wouldn't have been any busier on a nonholiday because all its businesses had gone insolvent and shuttered.

Only the corner deli was open. Its plateglass had just been washed and dripped with soap. The interior was hung with a backlit photomenu and shook with synthy snakecharmer pop. Past the sneezeguarded steamtray, an orb of meat rotated within molten coils.

Again. They were everywhere, it seemed. Arabs, Arabushim. Everywhere. On jobs, at the pumps, in the delis, at the rear of the delis down on their mats, and then up front behind their bulletproofed partitions wary, the third eyes of their prayer calluses keeping tabs on the aisles and mirrors and screens.

This one stood lanky and hairnetted, with a precipitous cleft in his chin to retreat to if anything went awry. And a moustache, that lip garnish that serves as an expression of some inner ambivalence: even if someone with a moustache is smiling, he's also always frowning—the mouth can turn up, but the hairs point down.

Uri grabbed Red Bulls and asked in Arabic for a pack of Marlboro Reds and the proprietor guy asked back, "You are from Jordan?"

"Palestine," Uri said.

"Hebron?"

"Gaza," Uri said, "but my friend is from Amman."

The proprietor guy nearly pounced across the register, pelting Yoav with entreaty: "When did you leave? Who's your family?"

Yoav stammered—a few gurgles to get a word, a few words to get the order, the effort coming to seem not like that of a man who spoke a child's Arabic, but like that of a manchild who hadn't spoken to anyone in a while, Arabic or not.

Uri intervened: "My friend has shoes in his head," which meant that Yoav was mentally disabled.

The Marlboro Reds and Red Bulls were regular price but the sahlebs they got were hot and gratis.

"Happy New Year" was the only English that was said.

The neighborhood was brick. Then it reverted to a vinyl that mimicked wood. From houses that could've been in TV sitcoms by day to houses that could've been in horror films by night, their materials might've quarreled, but their styles jibed: horrible, provisional. They were united by their provisionality, with their frontyards just fenced receptacles for trash and the trashed empty lots between them cast in the shadows of future buildings: highrises partially risen and a few so low they were just pilings or hadn't yet even broken ground.

They passed the candles and roses of a makeshift memorial to someone who'd died.

Capitolina Court was the street, a glorified driveway of a oneway one block deadend backing onto a defunct factory. One side of the street was a construction site's hoarding, each board of which was branded BAM: Bower Asset Management. The opposite side was only half vacant but weedy with what might in another season have been a berry plot. Next to that and set back from the street was a house that showed no address but had to be the address: an immense battered box of moldy whitewashed wood, summited by a spired gable like the red pin that marked its location on Yoav's phone. Except the gable was tilting and smothered in vines. The porch sagged bellylike from off its columns. A greasy Afric flag flapped from the letterslot like a doused rag to the cocktail Molotov. Nailed was the wishful sign, No Soliciting.

It was just after noon on New Year's Day, which meant doublepay. First of the month was first of the month, no exceptions, and the house had to be cleared before the developers snarled up for the workweek in their bulldozers.

Tom Gall, without having to realign and regear but just with a single curbclearing steer, reversed a rolloff truck into Capitolina.

There are few things in life more impressive to witness than a large vehicle being backed into a small spot—Uri, whether or not this had anything to do with the pill still in him, stood in the weeds wrapped in his shearling trying not to cry.

Tom raised the bed and Yoav stumbled over to help roll off the dumpster: a yawning rapacious 30 yarder they winched down flush with the gutter. They maybe shouldn't have been blocking the hydrant like that, but then maybe the streetlamps here should've been functional and the sidewalk slabs patched.

Go ahead, call the city and if you're ever taken off hold, report it—report everything: the day, the hour, the make, model, plates—the hydraulic hiss and wideload beep, the obstructing metal cauldron pitted and pocked, crusted with barnacles like a sunk submarine.

By morning its bottom would be dusted with frost.

———

Back under the Occupation, there had been shooting and here in America there was no shooting, or none aimed at them. Back under the Occupation, there had been sleepless stretches with nothing to eat and nothing to drink and here in America there were scheduled breaks and just a staggering range of fastfood options for both takeout and delivery. Also, in the IDF they'd been able to smash things. If they bumped into a Palestinian chair or desk or even human intact, they could smash it, they could call in a convoy of Doobi D9s to dismantle and raze, or a formation of F16s to fly in and cave the roofs and blast the walls into sand and sprinkle the foundations with phosphorous—but here in New York, they had to salvage.

Otherwise, the work they were doing wasn't too different.

They were still going into a house and checking the rooms by the floor. Checking for people, checking for possessions. Clearing the people before clearing the possessions. The possessions would stay with them, the people were allowed to go

wherever, provided it was always on the other side of the prop-
ertyline, which for this property meant anywhere past the skel-
etal hedge and remaining pickets of gateless fence.

Yoav had just been getting used to the normal jobs, when Uri
showed up and suddenly these new jobs, these eviction jobs,
were being put on the docket—which meant they had to pack
the people out to the street, but then had to be delicate packing
up the possessions.

They had to itemize everything, they had to swaddle it in soft
news and bubblewrap and pad it all safe away with foam, because everything was profit—because all possessions not re-
claimed King's Moving would get to keep and, as Paul Gall
always reminded, reclamation was as likely as identical snow-
flakes.

Some houses they'd strike it rich, some would be busts—
that was the gamble. That's why there'd always be a guarantee
of base fee from the landlord whose tenant they were tossing or
the bank or whoever held the lien.

Around Thanksgiving, they'd tossed two houses with nobody
home. In another residence they'd gutted, everyone was giddy
and civil because mentally feeble. Out in the Amboys, Tom had
been saying something that Yoav had been Hebraicizing for
Uri, something about how Uri's pay would be docked if he ever
broke another flatscreen, and as they were leaving the apart-
mentbuilding and passing the demonstrators with their ban-
ners, some woman, not an evictee but just some activist woman,
waved a deadly length of lumber attached to a placard in their
faces and chanted a slogan so passionately that she spit on
them.

Another woman had dandled her infant out a window and

threatened to drop it if anyone came in. Another had dropped a vat of sofrito, which scalded "Serbian" Phil and "Felony" Fredo Castro so badly they didn't work anymore, they wouldn't have to after they sued. Some guy neglected to mention the python he kept in a pantry—and Tinks almost—Tinks always almost.

In a tenement in Passaic, a woman had tried to bribe them, which hadn't made sense, that a woman who wasn't even making her rent was offering them cash to go away, but then what she was offering wasn't cash, she was just putting a pillow beneath her kneeling as Tom unzipped.

He finished in her mouth. "Swallow," he said. "Now get the fuck out of your house."

Here, on Capitolina, Yoav got into the truck and Uri, who was still slightly higher and drunker, followed. Tom sat at the wheel suiting up.

This was how they usually waited: all wedged together in the truck, not because the outside intimidated, but because it was cold.

Somewhere in Tom's wallet, somewhere plasticsleeved among the Amex and Costco cards and his CDL and DOT parking permit and DOB elevator inspector's certificate and the card that was always just a punch away from a free bagel, was a license that authorized him to seize property, including vehicles, and to perform evictions. Around his neck was a ballchain with tags and a bright novelty cop badge like a lemonlime airfreshener. He opened the glovebox and clapped on an FBI hat. Then he slammed his seat back and reached underneath and rummaged up a gun.

It was only when the Raelis—which was what Tom called them now that there was a pair of them, of Raelis—were around a gun that they realized they didn't have one.

Yoav said, "Explain me why we need that?"

Tom said, "You don't know where we are, Yo. You don't trifle with this neighborhood. Too many gangs, too many rival colors. I've had guys come at me with tirechains, guys with machetes."

"So only you need that and what I have? What he have?"

Tom said, "You're the Raeli cavalry."

Uri slumped away toward the window and clutched at a biceps through his shearling and grinned.

Tom shoved the gun into a pocket and turned up the heat and directed all the dash vents at himself. "Tell him, Yo, tell your habibi—this ain't Stapleton, this ain't even the Bronx, he can't be sloppy."

Yoav nudged Uri, "Tom's telling me to tell you to be careful."

Uri twisted around, "Careful of what—that SIG Sauer of his that's not even loaded?"

"It's not?"

"And if it's so dangerous here, why are we parked in front of the house and not around the corner? If we're raiding, wouldn't it make sense to sneak up?"

"It would. But we're not in command here."

"I'm not and you're not—he is, because your cousin doesn't trust us. Why else would that foreskin be our boss and the only one who's armed?"

"I don't know."

"Is anything about this kosher?"

"What do you think?"

Tom said, "What the fuck's he saying about kosher?"

"Unless I was just promoted in the field," Uri said to Yoav, "thinking's way above my rank."

Tom said, "You're going to stop hocking loogies and start talking English?"

Yoav, swiveling between languages, said, "Hocking what?"

"Fuck you and talk, what he was saying, your habibi."

"He saying he angry the others are late."

Tom checked his phone and rubbed at his sinuses. If only his employees—if only his evictees—would just do their jobs with the same dedication with which he did his, he wouldn't still be doing this, he'd have his MBA by now.

He'd spent New Year's at a kegger in Weehawken losing at poker and not getting laid.

Talc and Ronriguez honked their tractortrailer jacked halfway into Capitolina and Tom put the rolloff truck up on the curb to let them park.

Over break Ronriguez had paunched enough to have to loosen his backbrace out to the next velcro pad. He'd had so much family over, so many turkeyass meals, it was a joy, just about, to return to work. Talc had been down by his Virginia kin, coveting their acreage. Back in Jersey he'd winterized his garage and shut himself inside reconditioning the used lawn-mowers he'd purchased online.

They jumped from the tractortrailer cab to the street, Talc sleighbelling this crude ring of keys, and Ronriguez said, "You tell them."

"Tell me what?" Tom said.

"About this chica he with."

"Over break?"

"Late 80s, early 90s," Talc said, "and not a chica, this girl's pure shorty black, living like a stop away from here. I'm coming from wherever to hit that ass when this mugger steps to me from behind clowning me for cash."

Tom said, "He got a blade on him?"

"Damn fuck right a blade but I just be grabbing my ring like this, get the keys all up in my knuckles between them and spin around and puncture open his face."

Ronriguez said, "Híjole."

"Unlock the motherfucker's face."

Up on the porch none of the keys fit the paddy that well and as Talc riffled through the ring again Ronriguez was hassling trying to size up the bittings.

Yoav stomped alert atop the mats of soggy cash for gold ads, Any Condition Immediate Offer. Uri sounded out the weakest board and bounced.

"Is always smart of Paul to label which," Ronriguez said.

"Don't make no difference," said Talc.

Tom bounded back up from the rolloff truck with a crowbar and hooked its forktailed end under the paddy's shackle and leaning, slipping, regaining, pried the door with his weight. Wood cracked like it was breathing, releasing the ghosts from its grain. The shackle gave. The door swung and gaped.

Tom passed the crowbar to Ronriguez and, hand in his gun-pocket, passed inside.

"Mr. Luter?"

Across a sodden carpeting of circulars, menus for El Infante II and New Fu Shun, all shoeprinted alike with sawlike serrations split at the heel.

"Hola—la policía desahucio—Mr./Mrs. Luter?"

The planking and wainscoting flowed into the parlor under stainedglass panes of myriad greens, their tracery bent into leafshapes blown through by moted light. Growing up from out of the dimness was a miniature pine forest. A stand of miniature trees bristled against the holly patterning the wallpaper. A few others were leaned against the furniture, which wasn't pine but finer oak. The rest of the trees were laid by the hearth atop a wreathlike marquetry of cherry and maple. Beneath the raw tart pine scent were harsh stabs of mildew and camphor and beancurd rot. Tom picked up a pinecone and chucked it and wiped his hands of sap on a backpocket bandana.

They split at the stairs, Talc and Ronriguez going through to the kitchen and the basement below, Tom and the Raelis taking the top—Tom flicking at switches on his way up, though none of the tarnished sconces had bulbs. Down the gross shag hall, the rooms were like walk-in, live-in filingcabinets or bookshelves, clogged with yellowed paper.

Tom had the Raelis open each of the doors and then he came in behind them to open the shutters. The only upstairs room that seemed inhabited was the bedroom, which only seemed that from the twin mattress sheetless on the floor.

Otherwise it was as empty as the pillbottles, no labels.

The bathroom was wadded with napkins and cardboard toiletpaper tubes. Uri skimmed the showercurtain and yelled, "Incoming."

Tom hurried down the hall, "What?"

Uri yelled, "Radio clipped out, didn't copy—they're taking hostages, don't come in live but dry."

"What's going on?"

Uri stood over the toilet pissing. Yoav was laughing.

Tom flipped them both the finger. Uri flushed but the water was off.

Reports scrambled up from the basement: there was a bassinet (condition: Acceptable) and a pinball machine (condition: Poor). A black Virgin Mary garden gnome and a jumble of trunks swarmed with mice.

They all met up back in the parlor, under a pendant chandelier that hung like a churchlady's purse.

The parlor furniture was the stolidest stuff, of the same stately wood that varnishes courthouses and the lobbies of banks to instill the public's confidence.

Tom stood at the head of the dinette set and raised a halfpint of Hennessy in honor of whatever name resided on the paperwork—he'd forgotten it already. He passed the flask to Uri, who drank and passed it to Yoav, who after the others refused it just set it on the floor, because he wasn't sure whether Tom had brought it or just found it here.

"It's going to be a motherfucker," Tom was saying, "trying to get all this goddamned sap off the upholstery," and he went over to the pinepiled divan, tugged it back from the hearth. Trees fell away from the mantel. Roaches scuttled out of a carton of noodles. Charred logs toppled from the andirons. A hatchet gleamed from the ash. Black pleather orthopedic shoes with their sides cut to accommodate the swelling stuck out from under a quilt of Key Food bags and needles.

A syringe, crooked into the vitals of an elbow, fell out. The guy's face had been excoriated of shame.

Tom shook him by the shoulders but he wouldn't wake up or it was like he was refusing to be asleep or dead or anything at all but his refusing, and then Uri was down on the floor and putting an ear to his mouth and chest and picking up his eyelids and Yoav was down too with a hand on his wrist and uncertain whether the flurrying heart he was feeling was the guy's or his own or just Tom shoving in to rustle through the pockets. For the guy's no ID, for his no cash—Tom rolled him onto his side.

Tom told Yoav to get the arms, but Uri already had them and was lifting. Yoav picked up the hatchet and tucked it into the guy's blue uniform pants and covered its blade with the blue uniform shirt and Uri with his hands engaged could only judge, he could only scowl and oblige, give the guy if he were alive a fighting chance.

Yoav then hoisted the guy's legs and they ported him together out onto the porch and down the stairs with Yoav leading and so staking out the lower, the heavier, position. He found himself stopping, shuffling backward and stopping, to better his grip or let Uri better his, or just to give Tom the chance to reconsider: stopping at the roots that rived the walkway, stopping at the intermittency of fence, and Tom went on ahead.

The Raelis followed—taking the guy around the deadend's guardrail, thrashing through the grasses and out over the ice that reared the dilapidated factory.

They left the guy lying in the scant shelter of a loadingdock. Tom ran around to the front to get an address or name and had Yoav make the call on his Israeli phone, whose omnidigited number would barely register: "Just say you found a guy, back of Viamaris Bros., Spice Street at Nard."

911—Tom had to tell Yoav what to dial, but after that Yoav's voice held firm and before hanging up he even told the operator, "Thank you."

Back inside the house, they had just enough sun to clear the trees from the parlor, and then they nailed the door and left at dark.

Snow had started falling on the forest in the dumpster.

———

And it kept falling, contrary to every forecast.

All the predictions had the storm weakening after burying Jersey, but another front blowing down the Hudson collided with it and kept it trapped, blocking all the exits and boarding up the sky. The storm stalked around and raged and finally just dug in and squatted.

That night, the white came down on everything, came down equally. Driving hard, driving straight down, and as the winds shrieked like an ambulance down the cross streets what'd fallen was whipped up again, until even the blacktop felt as unstable as a cloud, like any step might be the wrong step, might be fatal.

That's what brought the kids out. The risk.

On TV, that teacherly white meteorology lady spraytanned to an indeterminate race had confirmed: school was officially cancelled.

The kids mustered on corners, they gathered at the tops of the overpass stairs, to sled down the smoothed enslopements atop trashcan lids, hubcaps, and flatpack cardboard. They outfitted a quadbike with a towrope and towed each other atop sheets of tyvek, scudding for flips and wiping out. They made idols of themselves and outfitted the idols in trashbag rags and enlivened them with features made of candy, chocolate eyes, fruit rings ears, mouths of Swedish fish.

They hurled snow at one another, and snow packed with ice, and snow packed with stones. Then ice and stones without snow.

The younger kids were called inside. Only a minor gang of the older kids stayed out and went throwing at the house.

The next morning Yoav and Uri were woken from dreams (about failing a squad equipment inspection) (about the former Finance Minister Yair Lapid parading Batya Neder on a leash down Boulevard Rothschild) by the reveille bells of the American phone.

Tom was just calling to say the job was still on and he wouldn't be picking them up.

Transit was running but only underground and delayed, so for a mile or three they walked it: dopey, haggard, glum. The sidewalks were indistinguishable from the streets and neither had any traffic. Stopsigns shivered in the gusts, stoplights flashed for no one. Christ would return to earth before this neighborhood got plowed.

The Raelis were greeted by a door like a jaw dropped open. All the house's windows were shattered into jagged vacancies caged by bars.

Tom was late and the Raelis were alone and cold and so exposed by the snow that it hardly felt like they even had each other.

Uri grasped a roughsnapped pinebranch from out of the snowjammed dumpster and mounted the steps to the porch. Yoav was just behind—"You're thinking there's someone inside?" and then, "If you're thinking there's someone, let's wait?"

Uri turned and put a finger to his lips and motioned with the pinebranch along the flanking fencelines.

"Uri, it's early and my stomach hurts. Let's not do this."

Uri shook his head and smacked, lightly but still tree-smacked, Yoav—sharp icicles across the cheek.

Of course Yoav hadn't forgotten, of course he hadn't misunderstood: how it went was that one team would go in the front and sweep toward the rear and one team would go in the rear and sweep toward the front—they'd meet in the middle and try not to annihilate each other. Though usually there'd be more than just a single soldier per team and more than two teams per house and snipers posted up on the roofs.

Yoav bootcrunched through the snowbank against the house's splintered siding. He wasn't going to surprise anyone, but then he wasn't even trying. The snow was immaculate and crusted with glass. Glary panes he ground into hoar. As he turned into the backyard, he was feeling that familiar, yet never familiar, unsettledness or flux, the approach of an unplanned-for, untrained-for moment, coming up like bile through the throat. That moment when no protocols apply and authority falls away, when anyone who acts becomes basically a general.

A whistle came in on the wind—Uri was giving a signal.

Then other voices were yelling, and not in Hebrew, as three kids in puffy parkas with their hoodies up and hitching up their jeans dashed out of the house by the knobless backdoor, two of them going around Yoav, but the middle one sprinting straight at him and knocking him down, just as Uri burst into the yard.

Yoav staggered upright and groped to restrain him, but Uri lashed out with the pinebranch and beat him back down and wailed, because the kids had already slid through a gap in the chainlink and split into the whiteness.

"Ben zonah, ben sharmuta, you can't even hold your position against a bunch of wasted kids?"

He huffed off to track them like a Bedouin in winter.

Yoav flicked the rime from himself and slunk inside.

The kitchen had been ravaged. The cabinets had been wrenched off the wall. Yoav was stepping on bowls, on plates, in shards. He was kicking bottles and cans across the smutted tile.

A skunkish stripe coursed along the hall. The mirror was sharpied, the pocketdoors jarred offtrack and sprayed: Da Fuck Off Our Block, 718 187 Fuck U Chaze BanKKK, BAM B✡WER, Kingz Moving We Gone Your House Now.

In the parlor, it was like a greedy hand had torn through the walls and brought the stainedglass of the transom crashing down. The staircase railing had been hacked apart, the landing was a mix of plaster and snow. Loosed bookpages swirled in the gusts. Up at the height of the house a pigeon flapped trapped under the skylight.

Coming back toward the foyer, Yoav turned into a gun. Tom had it leveled at his mouth.

Ronriguez and Talc were outside shoveling out the truck— yesterday they'd taken the rolloff but left the tractortrailer.

Uri stood in the street. Phonecalls were made, as Yoav hunched by the dumpster sucking air.

The house, left unattended for a single white night, had been defiled. By wilding children registering their fuck you. But fuck whom? The movers or the moved?

It might've been that even they weren't quite sure.

Every time Yoav glanced over, Tom was talking on the phone. Then Uri was talking too, but Yoav wasn't listening or whatever

Uri was saying got blustered around with the questions Tom was asking and Yoav was stuck between them: between Tom wanting a report, because his father Paul wanted a report, and Uri who by way of apology was telling Yoav about the first time he ever saw snow, when his family went up to Mount Hermon, where a sister of his was stationed briefly, all of them packed into the car with him sitting between his two other sisters forever as they drove lost through the Druze villages up in the hills, the only way the car could hold them all was because they were visiting Orly who was doing her service, and finally they got on the road they were supposed to have been on and drove as close as they could to the top, but had to stop at a checkpoint and they got out and stretched and his mother said, "Look, there's snow," and his father said, "Look, there's Beirut and over there's Damascus."

"You hearing me, Raelis?" Tom was yelling. "It's meeting time, come in for a huddle."

———

The situation was this: despoilment.

About half the take, the stuff—the furniture—was too far gone to move and store, because it was too far gone to monetize. There'd be no way to recoup. Not from a kneecapped wardrobe and brokenhandled chest. A cracked casement clock and leaky aquarium with just a hunk of polyurethane coral rattling around.

If this were any other contract, Tom said he'd drop it, or recommend dropping it to his father, but because this was the first contract from Bower, they'd stay. To protect the half of the assets left, to protect their reputation. Mitigate the loss. Fraunces Bower didn't hire heavylifters just to have them call the cops.

This was what Tom's father Paul was saying to everyone on speakerphone.

Reinforcements were being mobilized, though with Jersey in deepfreeze and the GWB unnavigable, no one was trucking in to roll another dumpster. Not until later today, at the latest tomorrow—whenever sanitation defrosted the roads.

Meanwhile, all the house's salvageable items were to be piled in the parlor, the rest was to be scraped and dumped out in the yard. No one was leaving—they'd be spending the night.

"Fuck that, Talc."

"Fucking hazard pay, Ronriguez."

The tractortrailer had an emergency kit: a gaspowered generator, a lightpod, and a spaceheater, which they set up in the parlor and Tom recharged his phone and Talc and Ronriguez took turns sharing Yoav's charger and each called his wife or girlfriend or whatever the status was of whoever it was who put up with him.

Then they put on their masks, but there weren't enough masks, so Tom tied on his bandana—they were already wearing their gloves.

They'd take the basement before the floor above, where the only light would be the sun that was left and the only heat that of their own exertion.

They worked their way through various techniques, from individual trips walking in and out to a chain passing the trashbags down to the sidewalk to the Raelis, who stacked them into an approximation of a barricade around the dumpster and propped them like bulging bodybags against the house's siding.

It was the repetition, that's what did it. What dulled. Bend, lift, throw. Bend, lift, throw. Run out of bags, get a new box. Run out of boxes, check the truck. Soldiers weren't supposed to clean up messes, they were supposed to make messes. "Yes, Uri." Soldiers made, they destroyed, what the others cleaned up. "Uri, yes." But what Yoav really said was, "Keyn, Aluf." "Affirmative, General."

What else was there to say? What did it mean that it was always easier to labor than to question, always easier to sweat than to ask? It dulled the mind but that wasn't all, it also dulled whatever muscle was responsible for judgment. What was effective, what wasn't. What was wrong and what was right. This was actually the most traumatic lesson of the army, that the most atrocious things they'd ever done were just the products of repetition. The missions, which had felt like maneuvers, which had felt like training scenarios, the footsteps were the same. One step after another. Feet concussing snow. His holes ahead of Uri's, through all that white sprawled out in front, sinister in its semblance, blank. Matching Timberlands, size 9 being an Israeli 42, half off for Christmas at Macy's. His boots printed the snow, which was so untouched and isolating that even after Uri had gotten his bearings by the minaret's moon risen over the impound grove and cut ahead to lead, Yoav felt like he was following a specter.

They'd volunteered to go to the deli, if the deli was open. Yoav had volunteered them, just to get out of the house and be doing anything different.

Uri stopped at a traffic median of work zone cones and took from his pocket a joint like a loosely rolled bandage and lit it with a lighter belonging to that bouncer Arik or that other club brother Zeev and puffed on it and handed it behind him.

The walk back was difficult. So far and so slippery, they were dizzy and burdened with too many bags.

Yoav kept dropping behind, so Uri stopped at corners to let him catch up and then Yoav wasn't catching up, so Uri turned and trundled to him and held out a laden hand and tried to disburden him.

"Don't, Uri. I got it."

"At least let me take the beer one."

"Don't touch me."

"The one with the beer—what's the matter?"

"Enough, it's cold. Yalla, kapara."

Uri went on and Yoav just after, but at the next corner Uri said, "I was only fucking around."

"That's what that was?"

"Come on, it was a joke, it was funny—you weren't laughing?"

"I laughed out of embarrassment."

"We scared him out of his kafiya."

"We didn't do anything—you did—but the guy wasn't scared. He's just a nice average guy, a Jordanian with a deli. One day you tell him I'm a retard, the next day you tell him we're mukhabarat, CIA agents investigating potential terror activities just wondering if he's noticed anything strange in the area and you don't think he got that we were Israeli? That you were being a prick?"

"You got all that with your basic course Arabic?"

"You're lucky I didn't speak to him in English and embarrass you."

"I don't put my dick on you," Uri said, which meant the same, in the obscure illogic of slang, as if he'd said that he did in fact put his dick on Yoav: the negative and positive versions of the phrase communicated the identical sentiment.

They slogged on, but crossing Spice Street, Yoav broke away and through the alley of Viamaris Bros. Uri, noticing the desertion at the curbcut, had to backtrack and overtook Yoav by the loadingdocks.

"What?" He was out of breath. "You expect him to still be here?"

"I don't even expect him to still be alive."

"He is—or was when we left him here." Uri swung his bags and chipped at the ice with his heel. "So what are we doing—just taking a shortcut?"

"Affirmative, General. That's what this is, a shortcut."

Yoav leaned against the loadingdock where they'd laid the homeowner, #3 it was. Or #5—Yoav couldn't recall, so he just alternated his attention between, as if trying to discern some remnant amid the irreproachably snowed cement.

Uri smirked, "You think there's something wrong with what we do."

"With what—getting high?"

"You know what I mean. Why do you act stupid?"

"I do? Maybe I act that way to avoid treating you stupid—maybe to avoid telling you what I think."

Uri tensed up, but he couldn't hit Yoav because his hands were full of groceries.

"If you want to hit me," Yoav said, "I can hold your bags."

Uri snorted and sucked some snot back into a nostril. "You're a cocksucker, you know that?"

"Uri, what if I'm not? What if you have no idea who I am? Just because we served together, that doesn't entitle you to anything. What I'm thinking, what I'm feeling. Did I shit today. How many times did I shit. Remember that? How we'd talk about shit all day and anyone coming back from the latrines, they'd have to give an update? How big or small their shit was? How many bombs they'd dropped or was it watery? Long and thin like a rocket, but a Gill or a Hutra? Or rounded like an M26 grenade, before or after fragmenting? And sometimes, or not just sometimes, we'd even check up. To keep everyone honest. We'd all march over to the ditch and crowd around in that stench standing over the suspect dump. Counting, evaluating, making sure no one got away with fabricating his payload. That's what I'm talking about, how fucked up that was. How fucked we got by the army. But, Uri, this is life. I don't need to tell you what's going on in my head or coming out of my ass now just to survive."

"OK, so if this is our life, what are you doing with it? The same as me."

"No, not the same. Because I'm trying to be alone here."

"That's why you have me living with you, working like a slave for your thief cousin and a goy amateur named Tom?"

"Like I said, Uri, I don't have to tell you anything, but one last time, I will. One last. I'm just trying to have a thought. A thought that the moment I have it my family or Sami or Eli or Natan or you aren't popping out of a mousehole to take it away from me."

He put his bags up on the loadingdock, Uri set his down in the wet.

"OK," Yoav said, "you haven't experienced this yet, but here's what happens when someone finds out you're Israeli. Someone from America, I'm talking about, even an American Jew. Either they say (he said this in English, in the voice of a young American girl), Oh my God it very horrible that the Palestinians they hate you and do to you the violence. Which means (he said this in Hebrew), Israel might be horrible, but at least all that violence lets you live a true Jewish life. Or they say (and again he said this in English, in the voice of a young American girl), Oh my God you have such privilege because you can leave from that not legitimate apartheid state that she make you to do the military service. Which means (and again he said this in Hebrew), You're so lucky you're able to quit that country founded on an obsolete nationalism devolved even further into racism and the massacre of innocents, I can never be your rehearsal partner for the audition or touch your penis, you're so evil."

"OK."

"Not OK, because I'm not that person—not the Jew to pity, not the Israeli to condemn."

"Yoavik, forget it—stop talking like you're fainting. Whatever we did in the army, it's done. If we were right, we don't get credit. If we were wrong, we're not responsible."

"But I'm not just talking about the army, Uri, I'm talking about everything. It was always just following orders. To be an Israeli is to follow Israeli orders. To be Jewish is to follow Jewish orders. Work follows work orders. Friends follow friend orders. Yoav follows Yoav orders. Uri follows Uri orders."

"So what? Whose orders would you rather follow?"

"We've always just been forced to become who we are and still everyone has an opinion about it, treating us like we chose this."

"So you're ashamed of who you are?"

"Everywhere we go we're Israelis, and if not that, we're

Jews. Everywhere we're the Jews of Jews, and if you think Palestinian is the best cover identity to assume—you know what they say: if your mother had balls she'd be your father."

"And if you had balls too you'd be a man."

"And the thing is," Yoav went on, "the only way I can separate myself from it all, in the minds of other people, even in my own mind, is to admit to what a piece of shit I was as a soldier. A big small piece of clusterbomb shit, already blown by the time I joined up. So answer me this: how did it happen that we were put in the same unit? Why did I get the same assignment as you, given my incompetence?"

"What can I say, Yoavik? That God fucks up and we call it a miracle?"

"All my life I pleased my mother and did everything she wanted and meanwhile the one single thing my father ever wanted was that I serve in his old unit, but he never asked, not me, and for sure he didn't ask the army, but still I could sense it, I couldn't not, like how you sense an ambush that never comes but still you keep preparing for it anyway just so that if it ever does come you can claim your retaliation's been proportional. So I, like a good boy, I was always good in school, found myself changing, it wasn't a decision, just a change, and I found myself doing whatever I had to do to qualify, like I was qualifying for placement not just in the infantry but also as his son, and then when I did that, when I accomplished that goal and got my placement and my father didn't react, my father said nothing, or nothing beyond just gaping at me like he didn't believe me, or like he suddenly didn't believe in the integrity of the army, I was crushed. By earning a spot I'd become unfit for that spot. The effort it cost me wrecked me."

Uri honked out a mucus cusp. "What you mean is that you won, but then you gave up—isn't that it? It bothers you to win? It makes you have guilt?"

Yoav said, "And I wouldn't have realized any of this without leaving—the army and the rest of it. But then you show up, or you're pressed onto me and I can't resist thinking."

"What?"

"I can't help thinking."

"What, you coward?"

"That you're what I'm trying to forget."

Uri hunched toward Yoav, who withdrew, and he gathered Yoav's bags and then gathered his own. "But you wouldn't be here if it wasn't for me," he said.

Yoav sighed. "And that's the worst of it for us both."

He tramped after Uri through the snowtamped weeds and around the guardrail onto Capitolina—stepping into a buried tire, almost falling from the softness onto the shoveled blacktop. The street's only light came from the house, leaking out from around the faces of cabinets wrested from walls and nailed across the windows to keep the wind and other trespassers out. The frontdoor had been hinged back on and wouldn't give. Yoav knocked with a boot. Gyorgi pried the nails from the inside with a crowbar and then exchanged the crowbar for a sledgehammer and renailed the cabinet face across the door to seal it shut. So Gyorgi was here and Grio was too and had brought tupperwared goat stew and leftover rolls and Absolut from some hotel buffet that some familymember of his was responsible for replenishing, which booze was chilling in a bucket of gutter snow set in the hearth. Uri unloaded the Coronas and Negra Modelos onto a tarp spread in the parlor. "Who got ham?

Who the cheesesteak?" Yoav was hurling out sandwiches and cheesecurls and pretzels and chips pulvered to salt.

Tom toasted their picnic. "Feliz Navidad."

Ronriguez said, "Is all you blancos know. Bet you $20 none you know how to say Happy New Year."

Tom said, "That's your toast, vato? I'm the only blanco here."

Gyorgi said, "Feliz New Year."

Tom said, "A merry jolly Hanukah, Yo?"

Ronriguez said, "$20."

Talc said, "To the holiday season."

Tom said, "To euphemism. To secularism."

Talc said, "I be raising to raises, to extra vacation."

Yoav said, "L'chaim."

Uri, as if this were a competition, chugged his beer and flattened it on his forehead and then nabbed Yoav's beer, chugged it down to the floor and did a pushup atop it, two pushups into it—three was what it took him to flatten it with his forehead, now marked by the rim and sopping with foam.

They smoked Marlboros—Tom's Camel Lights order had slipped Yoav's mind. They'd boarded themselves in so well they were clouding up the parlor.

Talc was crowbarring loose any paneling that was graffitied and Tom said, "We're going to have to sacrifice the mirror."

"That's bad fortune to smash it," Talc said.

"Worse not to smash it—we can't leave any traces. We tossed a guy out into the cold yesterday."

Talc said, "Why you sweating some crack bum? That guy ain't no owner."

Tom said, "We can't have our names here on anything."

All the surfaces that wouldn't be pried, like the wainscot, Ronriguez slammed out of the walls with the sledgehammer.

Grio had to piss, so Gyorgi removed a board from a window and suddenly everyone had to piss and the window was left unsealed.

Yoav and Uri were sent upstairs to gut the shelving.

It was too dark to demolish up there—they had to strip the titles and by touch alone puzzle them into boxes. Books of all sizes that if gripped by their spines felt like they'd never open and Yoav wondered, if he hadn't known they were books, what he'd think they were. Patio paving slabs, BLTs in clingwrap. As they worked, Uri kept bumping up against him. They'd roll each box to Gyorgi on the landing, who'd tape it and roll it to Grio on the bottom step, to stack.

Tom's phone rang and Tinks was told to go around. Tom helped him up and over the sill. Mind the puddle. The piss window was reboarded.

Tinks was fuming: he had an installation to dig out but instead he was here.

"An installation of what?" Tom said.

"Fuck you of what. My piece."

"Your piece of what?"

"My multimedia immersion art thing about climate change I've been fucking spamming you about since fall. The speaker consoles and stands for the holograms, my partner left them up on the roof and they got buried."

It was never obvious in his reference to a partner whether he meant that in the sexual or just artistic collaborator sense or both.

Anyway, Tinks had flaked on her or him and as he twitched off his backpack he said, "No fucking cabs out and I don't appreciate the threats."

"Don't get me wrong," Tom said, "I'm grateful you came. We're trying to stay energized—just tell me what I owe."

Tinks bounced a doppbag between his hands and said, "Fuck it. As long as I'm blowing off my projects."

Tom said, "As long as you're trying to keep your job."

Tinks said, "Clock me at rate from whenever you started to whenever we're done."

Tom said, "Done."

Tinks reached into the doppbag for a vial and said, "And everyone's going to have to roll me a bill. Make it $20."

Talc perked up. "You do how you do, Tommy G, but you're covering Ronriguez and you're covering me."

Ronriguez said, "Próspero Año Nuevo, chupacabra."

Tinks said, "Zion in the house?"

Tom said, "Upstairs," and then had the Raelis toss down ransacked books unboxed. Gyorgi tossed to Grio, who handed to Tinks who said, "Not the Koran," and Tom said, "*The Communist Manifesto? A History of Vietnam?*"

The back cover wasn't black & white—it was red, so became dusted in white, granular drifts of cocaine and whatever other substances might get subsumed under that rubric: babypowder, baby formula mix, vitamin B-12.

The Raelis were called downstairs and Uri knocked past Yoav, nearly sending him off the derailed landing.

Talc was rolling one of Tom's $20s and quizzing Ronriguez, who was rolling up the other, on who's the ovaled president: "Lincoln, who you fooling?"

They did their lines.

Tom said, "Who say you, Yo?" and Yoav said, "Gyorgi Washington?" and Tom mouthed a wrong answer buzzer.

Tom said, "It's up to Uri to restore our faith in the brains of his race," but Yoav had stopped explaining and Uri flexed his brow.

Tom squeezed another wrong answer out of his nose and had a line himself.

Tinks said, "That'll be $20 from each of you," and Yoav was certain Uri understood at least that, but neither of them reached for a wallet.

"What's up, Raelis?" Tom said. "You lovers got squabbles?"

He reached for his own wallet. "Fuck it, they're on me. Everyone's on me. Just trying to keep the fucking peace up in here."

He floated another two bills toward Tinks, tightened the one he already held like a screw. His phone, recharged to all bars, he untethered from the generator and, setting it atop a book box, he poured out the vial along the thumbsmudged screen. With his King's Moving Amex he tapped out a trinity of lines and called the Raelis from opposite corners of the parlor. But he didn't let them have any of the coke—just groomed and regroomed the graywhite gunpowder.

"You've got to earn your line," he said. "Answer my question and get a sniffle—understand?"

Yoav was throatclogged and about to demur, but Tom said, "Not you, I mean Uri. I know your answers, I don't know his. Jew my questions and don't fuck them up. Has he ever killed anyone?"

"I won't say that," Yoav said. "He won't answer."

"Let's try that again—I ask you and you ask him, that simple. Uri, have you ever killed anyone?"

Uri said, "You're too much of a pussy to tell me what he's saying."

Tom said, "What the fuck did he say to you?"

Yoav said, "He said I'm too much—afraid."

"Correct," Tom said and proffered his phone. Uri took the tuberolled bill, bowed his head and sucked a line. "That's enough. One at a time. Next question. Did you ever kill anyone in your own unit?"

Yoav refused, just shaking his head.

Tom said, "I mean by accident, of course."

Talc said, "Lay off him, Tommy G."

Ronriguez said, "He going to murder you."

"Or else," Tom said, "did any decision you made—like any managerial decision—result in the death of one of your own people?"

Uri asked what Tom was asking, but like he already knew.

Tinks said, "You have to be careful, Tom, referring to their own people. Because technically both they and their enemies are Semites."

Uri took Yoav's face in his hands and held it and Yoav rendered speech and Uri spoke and Yoav translated—he didn't interpret: "He said he sleeps now."

Tom said, "Not on this he won't," and Uri pinched a nostril.

Uri had this peculiar way of pinching a nostril: just extending a finger and pressing it in, then hunkering down with the bill.

Coming up for air again, he said in the first English he'd spoken like the first English ever spoken, "I sleep."

Tom said, "Last question. What about you, Yo—ask him what kind of soldier were you?"

Yoav was frozen but Uri was riled and put a hand to Yoav's neck and the inquiry passed between them—the inquiry and the reply.

And then the Raelis were rolling on the floor.

It wasn't even a tussle, just a barely completed roll, a pinning.

Yoav was trying to butt with his head but Uri butted him down gently, obnoxiously gently, grinned and quit him.

Yoav was up a moment later with the sledgehammer in his hands—raised to the chandelier's stripped sockets, twined to tinkle with its chain—he wasn't decided on what he was going to do with it. Just hold it. Wave it. Bring it down. Not to make contact, just wind in descent. But Uri, who had his back to Yoav and was heading across the parlor, crouched down for the crowbar and pivoted, catching the hammer midswing, bar against shaft breaking the swing, and then Uri was sliding the bar up the shaft beyond its point of fulcrum and, with a lunge, he forced the hammer high again, forced it high over Yoav's head, until Yoav was outfulcrumed himself and lost his balance.

Gyorgi stepped toward the foyer out of range, Grio backed toward the window that'd become the bathroom trying not to trip over the charger cord strangle. Talc and Ronriguez were leaned by the hearth just gawking.

Yoav was having to screen Uri out: two-hands-in-two-places (holding something with hands at either end) was better than two-hands-in-one-place (holding something with hands next to each other). Blocks beat swings, but then blocks were swings.

The horizontal always beats the vertical. There was no such thing as defense, just another's offense converted. Even if you weren't holding a weapon, even if you just had your hands, it still took a grip at two points to disarm an opponent. And just like with a weapon, it helped if you gripped your opponent at the poles: at two points, one on either side of the axis of symmetry—the farther the points, the stronger your grasp.

"Yo?" Tom said. "What's he telling you in Jew?"

Uri charged, and it was like training again, because training too had just been organized taunt.

Uri was going meanly tender, a strike and a withdrawal, strike and withdraw.

Yoav deflected, but after an errant sledgeswing split a floorboard, Uri got his boot over the hammer's head and held it weighted down as he thrust the forktailed end of his bar up against Yoav's scar, just below his throat.

"The adversary is his own adversary," he said, "because he's also your tool."

He ran the bar down Yoav's chest, his belly, the onesie's elastic.

Tom said, "Yo, you alright? What's this fuckhead up to?"

"Imagine a line at the center of your body. Divide your body in half."

"Fucking Raelis," Tom said as he blundered his gun out. "Get over yourselves already."

"To take you down," Uri said, "I have to apply more pressure to one side, less to the other. I have to apply contradictory pressures, pull you to one side, push you to the other. Whatever I do, I have to break your body at the center, each half going different directions. All attacks must reach to both sides of this line."

Uri stepped off the hammerhead and resumed the stance. "Kus emek—ready?"

Yoav shook.

Tom came between them and trained the gun on Uri. "Enough."

Uri said, "You enough."

Tom closed in and cocked the gun within bar range. "Drop it."

"Shot," Uri said. "Shoot."

"I will."

"Shoot me."

"Don't bog."

"Tom," Yoav said from across the parlor, "you don't think he knows it's not loaded?"

✳

The thing about following a star is where do you stop. Hard to tell where it's telling you to lay down your burden. Because a star can always seem to be above everything, it can always seem a block beyond. All you can do is follow until you've fooled yourself. They'd kept him overnight at Jamaica hospital and now it was the next night already and the translucent shackle on his wrist didn't have his name on it, just the date of the day he'd missed. Or else that was today's date.

From outside the Liberty Tax Service off Atlantic, he'd taken a jug, a refillable watercooler specimen.

The Shell station wasn't busy. He set the jug over by the garage and covered it with snow and with his wet hands washed his face and chimed inside, past the jamb's heightstrip that took his measure at 5' 9". CCTV cameras mounted in domes hung like teardrops cried by the ceiling. A sandwichboard advertised how slippery the floor was. The aisles were slushy and bootgrotted, clumped with Ford floormats and lined with aluminum racks stocked with antifreeze and jerkies and nuts. The lighterfluid and all other flammables were back by the beverage cases, whose coolingfans buzzed in opposition to the buzzing of the heatingvents and fluorescence to produce that same deranged Da Nang helicopter sound as can be obtained by driving fast with all the windows rolled down just a crack.

Directly behind the sandwichboard was a nativity display: a little fiberglass manger hut with a little plastic burro and a little plastic cow and a little plastic mother and a little plastic baby Christ cozened as if crystal, a fragile shipment atop a thatch of packing straw. Where was the little father, though—the husband whose wife Yahweh porked? Where were the little kings?

The magi: one of them was black, the others were white or Arab. The guy behind the counter was just a Shell uniform— "My boss, hello, what you want?"

All the containers Imamu was browsing were too large. He didn't need the fluid for BBQ grilling, he needed the fluid for lighters—whatever would fit in his pocket.

"Hello my buddy?" The guy banged the counter.

Imamu reshelved the container whose label he was rereading, whose instructions he'd reread until they'd been memorized.

The guy said, "You want lighter or cigarette? I sell you loose."

Imamu groaned and approached. "I don't know."

"Then what you here for?"

Butane, naphtha, kerosene, sterno. "I's just checking out your Christmas scene," he said, "and it's a beauty."

"No loiter."

"Remind me again where all this goes down—Bethlehem or Nazareth?"

"If you loiter, you out."

"I think Bethlehem, but then why they go calling him Jesus

of Nazareth, not Jesus of Bethlehem? What happen in Nazareth that it gets to name him? He don't die there, so he don't get resurrected there and anyway what's more important than where you first born? Or is it just that Nazareth's for the fancy folks and Bethlehem be ghetto?"

"If you don't buy, you go."

"Matches."

The guy slid out a pack and Imamu said, "More?"

"Go away from here."

He scuffled on, lugging the jug along the snowy humps between the curb and the galvanized mesh. No way he turned was the wind at his back.

The Gulf station's logo was a strange impotent sun split in half. Strange that the sun was also a star and that what the stars were made of was fire.

Carols blatted from speakers nested high in the shine of the canopy, salt sacks lined the apron by the pumps. Imamu waited by the employees only bathroom. All the parked vehicles were diesel. Then a paralytic transit van turned in to fuel and an attendant fitted the nozzle and returned to the booth, leaving the gallons and prices to cycle hypnotically until the driver's head was reclined and his turban had become like a pillow.

Imamu shuffled ahead holding the jug behind him, pressing it against the tomahawk tucked at his waist, the blade pressing cold against his ass.

He settled the jug down below the van's tank and reached for the nozzle.

The attendant burst from the booth waving an orangemawed shovel. "You trying to siphon me, mister fucker?"

Imamu said, "Me?"

"You come by again mister fucker I call the cops."

He backed away and at the closed BP station down the block, he hacked off a section of pressurized airhose.

He'd have to do this on the street, north-south streets numbered through the Conduits, narrower and with just the crescents of their corners lit by moon. He put the tomahawk to a vehicle's tank and busted its hatch. He loosened the cap and plumbed the hose on inside and stuffed a bootrag around it. The other end of the hose went between his chapped lips and he sucked. The vehicle was an old model Voyager. His lungs were old model lungs. He sucked until he tasted that sizzle, that tingle of gums contracting, teeth left to tumble from out of the skull. With a minimum of spillage he transferred the hose to the jug and stood above the trickle of bilious green.

Back on his block, Imamu doused the dumpster and poured a strip to the sidewalk and up the walkway onto the stairs. He wasn't worried about the porch planks creaking, he wasn't worried about being detected. With all the noise, the shaking. The house was being shaken apart from inside.

Then Imamu went down the lane again, doused the tractor-trailer and tomahawked its tires. He poured a last viscid portion to the blade, struck a match, and set the sharpness blazing. He touched the blade to the truck, which flared, and touched the porch and incited the stairs and then tossed the tomahawk atop the dumpster. And ran. That had always been his plan, the running, but now it was also his instinct. He skidded at midstreet, heaved himself up with blood warm in his mouth and hobbled away into the white bare bushery and through a gap between slats in the construction site hoarding and turned and lay facing the street.

A crane's boom crossed shadelessly over him. Behind him was a cementmixer. Behind him were girders. A pit.

A smoldering rat slithered up from the roiled guts of the dumpster and leapt from its ledge, landed on the street as if stunned and tailchasingly flipped over and over—like it was rolling around trying to snuff its fur—until it righted itself and stayed righted and scurried, vanished under the guardrail's metal horizon.

Within moments, the porch had caught and was becoming impassable: the wind was blowing all the balustrade's posts into votives, lit sticks dripping like wax. The door was veiled in fire and then the porch's planks collapsed and took the burning stairs down. The trashbags heaped between the walkway and sidewalk were sparked and their plastic blistered and peeled and flayed away from around batts of insulation glowing incendiary. As acrid flashes surged over the hacked stacked tables and a tangle of chairs, whose limbs were extended in a last flagrant plea, the hulking brazier of the dumpster roared.

It was like that account he'd read in—but Imamu was getting his books confused, their wisdoms twisting in his mind and becoming as difficult to sift and reassemble as ash—that account in the Koran or maybe some hadith or maybe some sermon that called hell the Abode of Fire, where sinners are chastised by the flames they called lies, where the blood of the sinful serves as fuel inexhaustible.

And from that dwelling, there came a knock—a knock from the wrong side of this house without a door—from the death side.

After having tried so hard to seize his house, the eviction djinns now were clamoring—they were chopping, slashing, banging, squealing, in what had to be an eviction djinn dialect they were squealing—to leave it.

They'd do anything to get out, even demolish it.

Suddenly, a cabinet or handled drawer board burst from a windowframe to the east and a murky bandanafaced figure boosted over the sill.

A black guy followed and then another guy who might've been Mexican but was as black as anyone in all that sooting, limping off into the darkness beyond the dumpster's candent rim.

Then two others followed—or three others—or four—rushing around yelling or coughing into phones.

A guy whose backpack had gotten snared on a nail dangled from the sill like a flopped parachutist. He writhed loose from his straps and strained his sneakers toward a drainpipe for footing and with his mohawk frizzling, he jumped.

Just then the columns that propped the porch's roof melted away and brought down an avalanche of shingling.

The bandanaface who according to his hat was also FBI stood panting by the deadend among the tires. He reached into his jacket and took out a dark snub of gun and wiped it down with snow and placed it, didn't drop it, but placed it, in a trashcan that he relieved from the freeze and tugged around to the back of the factory, leaving it with the dented mufflers and pallets and weeds.

The burning tractortrailer erupted into the accelerant wail of its alarm system.

In the lot to the west, two shadows were casting circles around each other, until the wind switched direction and sent up flares from the house to individuate their flesh.

The taller one was dredging a sledgehammer through the snow around the shorter one who wielded a crowbar to check under shrubs and disperse the trash, as if someone was crouching between the treestumps, as if someone was concealed under the berryplant cages and bent doorscreens—he was trying to smoke them out, whoever was responsible for this fire.

The taller one was closing in on the shorter one, but slowly, staying always at a smiting's length, brandishing the sledgehammer like a shepherd's crook and talking all the while—he was trying to talk the shorter one down. That was Imamu's guess, and Imamu had to guess, given the dim and his angle and lowness and that whatever was being said was in that Arabic that wasn't, that Arabic that hated itself, that mocked itself, that seethed, and took the air in whitehot puffs like sheared wool.

To himself, Imamu had been calling the taller one Big Djinn, though he wasn't bigger, just taller. He'd been calling the shorter one Little Djinn, though he wasn't littler, just shorter, and seemed the stronger, or seemed aggrieved enough to be.

He, Little Djinn, swung around and clashed his bar into Big Djinn's hammer and beat him back across the lot littered with winter until he had him trapped up against a solitary section of chainlink fence blown slanted from a snowdune. Big Djinn was stuck, so Little Djinn struck, and barred the hammer from his grip. Big Djinn fell into the chainlink and cowered, covered himself with his disarmed hands and then fumbled in his pockets. But instead of finishing him off with the bar, Little Djinn picked up the hammer and lifted it too, as if to finish him off with both. He was holding both high and crossing them and whetting them against each other to prime, as Big Djinn raised his hands with what he'd taken from his pocket. It was a flashlight, and its stray spot of flame caught the face that raged above and froze it in its agony.

This was what Imamu witnessed, what he understood. The rage that lacked an enemy. The voice that lacked for heed. Little Djinn brought the bar and hammer down, hitting the edges of the fence, which shook beneath Big Djinn like a rusty web.

As Little Djinn stalked away the flashlight's target flickered at his back and the shrieking built to the keening pitch of sirens.

Fire was on the scene before the cops, but could hardly fit their engines onto Capitolina, could hardly even make the turn to roll up on the lots.

Fire had bigger axes than Imamu ever had. But Imamu wasn't sensing their danger.

It was the shorter guy who was the danger—the stark swart compacted guy he'd been calling Little Djinn who was rushing back and forth along the length of the hoarding, clearing the bushes with the bar and hammering at hedges, but haphazardly, madly, like he'd gotten muddled as to whether he was still trying to find someone to punish or just becoming that someone himself. Others were putting their hands up, putting them down on the hoods, legs spread, or they were running, or being run after, Imamu couldn't keep track, he couldn't tell who was who, given how the cop uniforms and the uniforms of the evictor djinns matched in their blues and how the plownosed cruisers paralleled up on the curb stirred the smoke with their rotating red beacons. Red the color of the coldest flame, blue the color of the hottest flame, white the color of surrender. The cops were yelling as Little Djinn kept hitting against the hoarding and cracking its slats and Imamu felt the cracking in his bones. Big Djinn was out in the middle of the street flailing uncontrollably like a scrawny hose and spewing that gritty particulate language, like he was spitting out the teeth that had to be crushed to speak it, but whatever he was saying wasn't defusing. The cops had their guns leveled and were yelling over the spray, "Down, put it down." Little Djinn swung the bar and hammer in circles to fend them until he was spinning like the chief dervish of a springtime cult beseeching heaven. "Freeze, you fucking raghead." But Big Djinn dashed between the cops and their aim and said in English, "He don't speak English." The cops whipped around, "Show us your hands." They weren't sure what it was in his hand. "Weapon, weapon." "What're you holding?" "A light." "What?" Someone yelled, "It's just a fucking flashlight," and Big Djinn raised and shone it and roved around its beam. "Goddamnit put it down." Someone yelled from by the cruiser, "Best be cool, they army." Little Djinn was now just beating the street itself, striking as if tilling the iced hard intransigent blacktop of laneless Capitolina. "The both of you down or you're dead," this voice said, and Big Djinn clicked the flashlight and dropped it and was swarmed from behind and just as the backup cops were slicking him down with their knees in his back, Little Djinn lunged out swinging—so a cop shot him, so the other cops shot, each firing to empty for a share of the blame.

✻

Pete Simonyi was David's lawyer and so he was Yoav's lawyer too and he sought to reassure his client by speaking a grammarless Yiddish, which Yoav didn't know and the lawyer thought was Hebrew. He'd called Yoav's parents—at David's request, or Yoav's own, Yoav wouldn't swear to which—and reported that though they were hoping to speak to their son directly they were pleased for now that he was being represented by a Jew.

As for Uri's parents, Pete Simonyi said that the NYPD should've called them, or the ICE, the Immigration and Customs Enforcement, or the DHS, the Department of Homeland Security, or else officials of the Israeli embassy or consulate, and Yoav said that he, Yoav, should've called them himself. He'd been imagining Uri's parents being woken up by the news in an English that never was theirs.

Tammy had been with her mother, Bonnie, and Bonnie's husband, Carl, for Christmas. Las Vegas.

Their house was a splitlevel pseudo pueblo that commanded a culdesac in a half empty pseudo pueblo development. Inflatable candycanes were staked into the lawn level with the Bar-

bary pricklypear, but it was just getting tougher, it annually was, to ladder up to the vigas and string the lights.

Bonnie the aspirant cowgirl was still into lipo and botox and suede, but by this visit had also adopted a hat and this disturbing tic of chewing on its chinstrap, which made all her pronouncements drooly and incomprehensible.

Carl, tactful, escorted Tammy into the garage to show her a Trans Am he'd redone for a customer in Denver and ask her the same question he always: what kind of car was she driving now, the answer to which was still none.

She flew to Los Angeles for New Year's and met up with her boyfriend. They stayed in the Hollywood condo of a director friend from NYU off shooting on location. LA had its own local news, it didn't need New York's. She'd been in Malibu when her father had called. She'd been clenching her boyfriend from behind on a motorcycle ride down Laurel Canyon when Ruth had called. Her father hadn't left a voicemail. Ruth had, but just of weeping.

Tammy hopped a flight alone and now sat indignant across from her cousin asking whether he'd been brutalized by the cops or informed of his rights as an undocumented laborer. But what she wanted to ask was, "Do you know where my father's run off to?"

Yoav's jaw was sore, his head was gauzed, so that the only thought he had was: you have a boyfriend?

She took out her phone and showed him vacation photos.

Pete Simonyi got his client transferred from Varick Federal Detention to Hudson County Jail, a facility in Jersey. There they put him into yet another uniform, the color of Uri's face, which he'd identified.

Yoav sat on his bunk reading his cell's only book, the Bible, which would bring him no solace because this was its language and the version was modern.

———

They were in Mexico—Ruth had been after David to take her since summer. In the interests of his health. She'd extracted a vow while he'd been hospitalized, recovering from his heart. Nurses, doctors, insurers—all will pick your pocket while you're low, but only lovers go scavenging for promises.

"We're gone two full weeks," Ruth had told her exhusband Bill. "Only 12 days," David had told the office, which was what Ruth had told her son, Bill Jr.

The band that manacled David's wrist was jetblack and flecked with glitter. It entitled him to three meals a day, bottomless drinks, access to pools, stretches of beach, and unlimited free towels.

But he preferred hanging by the front of the resort, among the queuing shuttles. The driveway was a roundabout with an island of poinsettia and yucca and a golfcart decked like a Christmas sleigh hitched up to a team of piñata llamas. If the signal was good he sat in the golfcart like an offduty Santa, if it wasn't good he stood out at the extremities. He'd also tried the upper tenniscourts (but they had to be booked in advance), or over by the AC units (but their whirring interfered).

Anyway, they were the refuges he had—locations he'd found by trial and error to have the best phone reception at the resort.

Ruth complained about the frequency of his check-ins, so to assuage her David agreed to hold their New Year's meal out by the surf, with the staff having to move their table, chairs, and torches in with the tide.

They spent the remainder of the Eve in the jacuzzi, or he spent the remainder, to spite Ruth after she nagged him to get out, because jacuzzis exacerbated cardiac insufficiencies.

This was, she said, because of the temperature, but he could handle that—he could adapt. If anything was stressing him out it was the bubbles.

The day he was told, he told Ruth nothing. He wanted to fly yesterday, he wanted to rebook his ticket while still talking on the phone.

But Pete Simonyi said, "Better not."

"Explain that to me?"

"Better wait it out until we've assessed your liability."

He got sick or convinced himself he was getting sick from the bilge they washed the tomatoes in. From brushing his teeth.

He got burnt from staying out at the extremes of the drive-way all day. Just waiting on a call or for bars of service. Drinking bottledwater or the vodka he'd bribed the bartenders to fill his waterbottles with. Checking two timezone times on his phone, checking his wristband like a watch.

For the next four days, his conversations with Pete Simonyi were like teenaged contests over which of them was endowed with the bigger longer stubbornness—if David came now, the lawyer was saying, he might be arrested and charged.

"With what?"

"Schmucking."

"That a crime?"

"Aggravated schmucking."

"So you're saying no crime?"

"I'm saying the cops have a certain courtesy way of investigating cops, of covering for them. Investigating you comes next."

"How much it's going to cost me to make that not happen?"

"Bower was just asking the same question, how much it's going to cost you."

"Fraunces Bower called?"

"No, David. His lawyer called."

"So they're putting distance?"

"With an illegal handgun found on the scene?"

"Anyone knows whose it is?"

Uh Dugn knows. Now put on your sunblock and go inside."

He went inside, bypassing his own room to find the media-room and move its banquettes around to find an outlet to charge from.

But he'd lost his charger. Or Ruth had taken it. He went to their room and mussed around, Ruth hadn't. The charger had been coiled around his wallet all along, its cord weighted with its twopronged converter curling from his unzipped fannypack like the prehensile electric tentacle of something bad he ate.

He tried folding Ruth's clothes again and returning them to her suitcase but hadn't quite gotten every seam of negligee aligned before she came back from her manipedi and was accusing him of snooping, so he was accusing the maids of snooping, his phone tolled with expiring sighs, and Ruth thudded her bare flat gull feet and pink toenails into the bathroom and try as he might he couldn't convince her that he liked the negligee, and that he'd like her in it, or even just to unlock the door.

He'd failed as a lover and husband and father and cousin and now this—he couldn't even keep a phone alive.

He kept thinking Ruth knew, but he hadn't told her, even by Monday, 1/4/16. He kept thinking even the staffmembers knew—the waitress in the poncho who'd curtsied, the grounds-keeper in the armsling who'd winked, and that one lifeguard enthroned high up in the tower who kept singling him out for a pensive nod or smile from among that unctuous bloated gringo armada that daily sailed its whiteness past his vigilant mirrored sunglasses.

At the dining pavilion, La Hacienda, the manager must've searched David up in the reservations database and on what should've been David's last day made sure to stop by David's table and kept using David's name, asking if David needed more sopa, if David wanted more corn as opposed to flour tor-tillas, and offering to get David another flan just as David was swallowing the initial scoop of his initial flan and Ruth said, "David's had enough already but mucho mucho gracias, Ángel," because David was perspiring and kept popping his bathing-suit's snaps.

As they left through the lobby, the concierge whose name-tag's flag gave the excuse that he was Swiss stopped David to tell him it wouldn't be an issue—they could extend their stay, they didn't even have to change suites.

Ruth said, "What're you talking we're staying?"

David said, "Can we change suites anyway?"

Ruth said, "But you hate it here and I have a son," and then to the concierge, "No offense, but he hates it."

The concierge said, "And if I may ask, please, what is wrong?"

Ruth said, "This is who you're asking what's wrong?" and then to David, "What aren't you telling me?"

David said, "I was hoping to relocate to the class or price-point just below whatever it is we're in currently."

After the concierge checked the availabilities, he mentioned having noticed that they hadn't yet registered for any of the activities or excursions offsite—he was wondering whether David and his wife might be interested in touring the ruins, which weren't merely fascinating but precolumbian?

David said, "Not just now," and was drowned by his phone, whose ringtone he'd changed from Ether Funk to Hatikvah.

"Snorkel, scuba, hanggliding, parasailing."

Ruth said, "Wife?"

The concierge said, "Have I mentioned the ruins, which can also be done on horseback?"

Ruth snorted and went off to her facial.

David headed to La Cantina for cigs and a refill of his vodka-bottle and drank and smoked between a sandtrap and clay.

He returned to the room only after dark to recharge and found Ruth gone—her suitcase inclusive. Though she'd left his ticket on the bed. Atop it glittered a stretched and shredded ring. A plastic ring.

She'd had trouble taking off her bracelet.

———

The laws of the dead are for the living—who else is going to follow them?

Yoav?

The corpses of Jews have to be washed, they have to be wrapped. They have to be sat with around the clock. A Jewish corpse can't be left unattended, from the last breath to the last graveside spade of soil. A body unattended is a body unlocked, a doorway without a door—evil will just sneak into a cavity.

As for the burial, it has to happen the day after death or, if that's Shabbat or a holiday, the day after that. It can't wait until the World Cup's over or for cheaper airfares. For when the criminal suits cede to the civil suits, inquiries, probes. Or for when the verdicts are returned for the guilty and not.

Certainly not.

Uri remained drawered in the morgue.

Yoav's only visitor was a woman whose name, unyieldingly, was Dina.

This was the nature of their tribe: there was always a fair chance that the woman responsible for your fate had the same name as your mother. If he squinted he might even hear his mother's voice, saying she was visiting from the consulate, in New York, acting on orders from the embassy, in Washington.

To be spoken to in Hebrew was a relief, after all that inter-rogation in English: the language of consistency, the language of pertinence.

Yoav repeated his account and then asked about Uri, his body—Yoav's tongue pounding in his mouth like boots on the ground.

Dina told him that the body was evidence now and that while the law here routinely respected religion, that was mainly if not exclusively in situations regarding diet and clothes, and though a petition for release of the body could be filed, it couldn't be by Yoav, who wasn't next of kin. She consoled him with a courtdate and though she said she'd rather not specu-late, she speculated, and said he'd be deported.

"Where deported?"

"Israel—where else?"

He stopped himself from asking how his father was.

He dreamed he was on the plane already. Which was like still being in jail, the same amount of legroom, had to cramp your head down. He was bitched in the middle of a three-row between an older couple reluctant to request he switch and sit on the aisle. It was only when he'd recognized the flightattendants as being Uri's sisters that he recognized the older couple as being Uri's parents, despite never having met the lot of them. All the other passengers, being served pillows and meals and drinks by the flightattendants, were Dugris too. All the extended family. A reunion atmosphere prevailed. With relatives digging into foiltrays of steaming fleshes, coffee or tea, coffee or tea, soft beverages iced with 9mm rounds, clinking. Everybody was being served except him. Then everybody had finished and was standing, blocking the emergency exits and washrooms with chat, catchup, commiseration, and, during turbulence, and the flight was turning turbulent, they grabbed for one another, as 9mm rounds rolled down the aisles. Relatives, trying to return to their seats, were falling. Luggage rattled out of the overheads. The plane was upended and a riot of prayer. Yoav was one of two seated, harnessed. The hatch to the cockpit was ajar. Inside, Uri was sitting. Uri's dead corpse. He wasn't stowed down as cargo in the belly of the plane, but leaned up against the indicators, as pilot. He wasn't infantry anymore, he was flying. His chest was blown bloody open and his breastbone was the controls. His ribs had been opened and driven into the plane, had been welded and wired into the

plane, to become its yoke or stick, an intimate apparatus of its navigation. As he slumped, with loss of blood and altitude and speed slumped, the plane bowed its forehead to the earth.

The day of the funeral, Yoav slept late. Wrapped naked in a sheet with an army rapping at his door.

———

David had never been to town before, to this town, and only now understood why it wasn't one of the recommended excursions. It's not like the concierge was in a position to tell guests what to do when they weren't quite convinced of the wisdom of using creditcards.

He was trying to get interested in the sites, but after doing the church the only structure left was the fort, a decaying, colonial-era complex, all of which was closed except its giftshop and prison. He dropped an American quarter into the box, took the worn steps spiraling him dizzy to a dank chainbound cell—made it all the way up and down again in the span between bells.

He wobbled back to his pension, where dollars were accepted and passports weren't scrutinized.

Back to the room, one room, where every effort to forget himself ended in a nap.

He wasn't technically a fugitive, just loathed. All his voice-mails were from (212) SIM-ONYI.

When the sun went down, he went out to a restaurant, the one that hadn't yet made him shit, and sat on a steeringwheel stool reading the resort's copy of last Sunday's *Times*, eating soggy pork tortas and drinking tequila and mezcal until the restaurant had turned into a bar and he wasn't understanding even the paragraphs he'd memorized, the sentences were blurry and

he was drunk and white in Mexico and odious. The cigs here all scalded the tongue and were over too fast.

It was stupid to have come here, if not suicidal. An imperiled Jew should just jet to Ben Gurion and beg asylum, but that option wasn't his. He was a Jew who couldn't seek refuge in Israel. Who needed another Israel, who needed an alternate. So why not Campeche? La cuenta, por favor?

He took his second shower of the day, then gave the shower a bath, cleaning plugs of pork from out of the drain because he'd vomited.

He walked the streets, trying to recall the kaddish. Passing into slums, into fields. He was searching, vaguely, for the ruins. Not the ruins they'd tried to get him to horseride to at the resort, but other, lesser ruins—in the fort's giftshop, he'd noticed a postcard of them, a tiny formation of disintegrating pyramids and he'd asked where they were and the woman had tried to sell him the postcard, which David refused, and a map, which he already had.

He'd unfolded it and she'd pointed to where, a brown pyramid, which marked a site of historical interest, the storage of the dead. And it'd seemed walkable.

It'd seemed along this road—a road without Jews. The sun was sowing him a migraine.

He passed winnowed fields and a dusty closed store with a stilled barberpole out front fitted with a strip of rough cloth that might've been a severed pantleg or sleeve flapping to indicate the vagrance of wind and claiming all this territory under the sovereignty of the forsaken.

He met an old woman whose cheeks were studded with brown dotty moles and pointed at the map, "Piramida?"

"No sé."

The rest of the fort was slowly reopening after some holiday or scheduled restoration work that, if it'd been completed, he wasn't noticing, as he walked the ramparts and petted the cannon. He walked all the way around and then ducked into one of the battlements, some semicircular chamber shaded by a dome, and he pressed up against the slit between its stones, that mossy gap through which conquerors once shot fire. It wasn't much of a view, it was more of a defense than a view. All it gave was a sliver of water, which toward dusk was crossed by a boat.

✳

He wasn't acquainted with many at the masjid anymore. They weren't his folks, most. Their soupkitchen was unwelcoming and poison. The rest of the neighborhood had it in for him too, but he trusted it not to go snitching. He'd pay calls to his house, which had become just a lot, and it wasn't even evident which lot it'd been, because no traces of demolition remained and also, his brain. There were just two blocksize construction sites now, facing each other, hoarded faces expressionless, the machinations behind them concealed and, once he ventured behind their fencing, sedent, idle. So, anyway, the world was upsidedown. The world was turning backward. He'd be wearing his clothes in the regular way until they were soiled and then he'd be turning them insideout and wearing them until they were soiled again and except for the stitching the insideout and regular would be identical, and if the occasion was bundling in a storm drain or bedding down beside Spring Creek, whose icy rail flowed through the sewers of Brooklyn and into the train tunnels of Queens, he'd wrap himself in broken unspoked umbrellas. He slept by day so as to stay awake all night and use the cover of darkness for his errands. Pulling behind him a shoppingcart or, when that got snatched, pushing a heapy baby-stroller up over the ties, he'd surface from the tunnels. Under the attainder of all weather. Under the plundered light of the moon. His home had become the A Line, which plunged sub-terranean between the stops at 80th and Grant, past the wall of that red stone called bluestone behind the Chase Bank branch at Drew. He had a crack, a chamber, dry enough, patched with books from the library. The trains would pass just by his cheek, gusting cold. More on weekdays, fewer on weekends. His cal-endar. He remembered he had to go to the library, there was something he'd forgotten, something due. But he couldn't stand, he couldn't even sit up. Being hungry was like being hit but never feeling it, never feeling anything. He had papers in a bag for a pillow. He wetted his lips with the thaw. He lay on his side as a light like rising mercury rose up the rumbled track and a breeze bore him on to where there wasn't any winter.

✹

ABOUT THE AUTHOR

JOSHUA COHEN was born in 1980 in Atlantic City. He has written novels (*Book of Numbers*), short fiction (*Four New Messages*), and nonfiction for *The New York Times*, *Harper's Magazine*, *London Review of Books*, *n+1*, and others. In 2017 he was named one of *Granta's* Best of Young American Novelists. He lives in New York City.

ABOUT THE TYPE

This book was set in Caledonia, a typeface designed in 1939 by W. A. Dwiggins (1880–1956) for the Mergenthaler Linotype Company. Its name is the ancient Roman term for Scotland, because the face was intended to have a Scottish-Roman flavor. Caledonia is considered to be a well-proportioned, businesslike face with little contrast between its thick and thin lines.